A BEASTLY E

John Blackburn was born in 1923 in tl
the second son of a clergyman. Blackbu … ollege
near London beginning in 1937, but his education was interrupted by the onset of World War II; the shadow of the war, and that of Nazi Germany, would later play a role in many of his works. He served as a radio officer during the war in the Mercantile Marine from 1942 to 1945, and resumed his education afterwards at Durham University, earning his bachelor's degree in 1949. Blackburn taught for several years after that, first in London and then in Berlin, and married Joan Mary Clift in 1950. Returning to London in 1952, he took over the management of Red Lion Books.

It was there that Blackburn began writing, and the immediate success in 1958 of his first novel, *A Scent of New-Mown Hay*, led him to take up a career as a writer full time. He and his wife also maintained an antiquarian bookstore, a secondary career that would inform some of Blackburn's work, including the bibliomystery *Blue Octavo* (1963). *A Scent of New-Mown Hay* typified the approach that would come to characterize Blackburn's twenty-eight novels, which defied easy categorization in their unique and compelling mixture of the genres of science fiction, horror, mystery, and thriller. Many of Blackburn's best novels came in the late 1960s and early 1970s, with a string of successes that included the classics *A Ring of Roses* (1965), *Children of the Night* (1966), *Nothing but the Night* (1968; adapted for a 1973 film starring Christopher Lee and Peter Cushing), *Devil Daddy* (1972) and *Our Lady of Pain* (1974). Somewhat unusually for a popular horror writer, Blackburn's novels were not only successful with the reading public but also won widespread critical acclaim: the *Times Literary Supplement* declared him 'today's master of horror' and compared him with the Grimm Brothers, while the *Penguin Encyclopedia of Horror and the Supernatural* regarded him as 'certainly the best British novelist in his field' and the *St James Guide to Crime & Mystery Writers* called him 'one of England's best practicing novelists in the tradition of the thriller novel'.

By the time Blackburn published his final novel in 1985, much of his work was already out of print, an inexplicable neglect that continued until Valancourt began republishing his novels in 2013. John Blackburn died in 1993.

By John Blackburn

A Scent of New-Mown Hay (1958)*

A Sour Apple Tree (1958)

Broken Boy (1959)*

Dead Man Running (1960)

The Gaunt Woman (1962)

Blue Octavo (1963)*

Colonel Bogus (1964)

The Winds of Midnight (1964)

A Ring of Roses (1965)*

Children of the Night (1966)*

The Flame and the Wind (1967)*

Nothing but the Night (1968)*

The Young Man from Lima (1968)

Bury Him Darkly (1969)*

Blow the House Down (1970)

The Household Traitors (1971)*

Devil Daddy (1972)*

For Fear of Little Men (1972)

Deep Among the Dead Men (1973)

Our Lady of Pain (1974)*

Mister Brown's Bodies (1975)

The Face of the Lion (1976)*

The Cyclops Goblet (1977)*

Dead Man's Handle (1978)

The Sins of the Father (1979)

A Beastly Business (1982)*

The Book of the Dead (1984)

The Bad Penny (1985)*

* Available or forthcoming from Valancourt Books

JOHN BLACKBURN

A Beastly Business

VALANCOURT BOOKS

A Beastly Business by John Blackburn
First published London: Robert Hale, 1982
First Valancourt Books edition 2014

Publisher's Note – The 1982 Robert Hale edition, from which the present edition has been typeset, contained an unusually large number of typographical errors, often several per page. Every effort has been made to correct these errors for this reprint.

ISBN 978-1-939140-84-5 (*trade paperback*)
Also available as an electronic book

Published by Valancourt Books, Richmond, Virginia
Publisher & Editor: James D. Jenkins
20th Century Series Editor: Simon Stern, University of Toronto
http://www.valancourtbooks.com

Cover by M. S. Corley
Set in Dante MT 11/13.6

Preface

The Vicar called on Christmas Eve and he didn't stay long. His visit was not reported till the next morning and it was 10 a.m. before the police arrived.

"A slaughter house." The investigations had started when Inspector Pode came on the scene and the extent of the carnage shocked him. George Pode had often met Mary Blake and considered she was a rather handsome woman. No one would have called her handsome now. Her body looked as though it had been savaged by a wild animal or torn by a machine. The murderer must have spent some minutes in the bathroom washing off her blood.

"Number Six, eh?" Pode questioned a C.I.D. sergeant who was checking the contents of a desk. "Any doubt that it is the same blighter, Clarke?"

"Not to my mind, sir." The sergeant held up a wad of notes. "There's over a hundred quid here and twelve in her handbag. We can rule out robbery and Doctor Rant thinks sexual assault's unlikely."

"It must be the Vicar. That damned, bearded, uncatchable Vicar."

"We'll catch him, Clarke. We'll nail the bastard never fear." Pode spoke with a confidence he didn't feel. He had studied the files on the previous cases and the killer almost seemed to be protected by fate—certainly by lack of motive.

The police called the murderer *Vicar*, because witnesses had noticed a bearded clergyman leaving the scene of three of the crimes. At first Scotland Yard imagined that the clothes were a disguise and the beard was false, but the fourth victim proved them wrong on the second point. Number Four had put up a struggle and a tuft of coarse facial hair was found clenched between her fingers. Hairs pulled by the roots. Hairs of the killer.

A thick-set clergyman with a grizzled beard. An easy person to trace one would have imagined, but there were difficulties. The

Vicar roamed a wide area and chose his prey at random. London and Cardiff . . . Leeds and Glasgow and Newcastle. Young and old, dark and fair; tall, short and plump and skinny. All types interested the Vicar.

The other problem was that there was no apparent motive . . . No method in his madness. With one exception all the women had had money on their premises, but the Vicar had not touched a penny piece. Though two of the women had been prostitutes, the medical evidence suggested that sex was not the Vicar's aim. He had just knocked on a door and killed the woman who opened it.

"Weapons, Doctor Rant?" Pode turned to a police surgeon craning over the corpse. "A knife and a hatchet as usual?"

"Yes, Inspector, and probably three others, though we can't be sure yet. The doctor stood up and pointed at an object on the floor. "I'd say he used a chisel and some round instrument as well. Maybe a rat-tail file or a marlin spike, but that's the actual murder weapon."

"A crucifix!" Pode grimaced at the heavy brass cross. "He brained her with a crucifix before starting work."

"Her own, sir." A young constable spoke. "Miss Blake was involved in a minor motoring accident last year and I came round for a statement. She was a Catholic and the cross was over there, hanging beside the mantelpiece."

"The bastard!" Pode was a Catholic himself and he felt a sudden personal hatred towards the murderer. "Why?", he muttered, turning to a window as a chime of bells started to celebrate Christ's Nativity. "Why . . . what makes him tick? Why bring along a bag of tools to mutilate the bodies? Doctor Rant considers Miss Blake was dead or unconscious before he carved her up and so were the others."

"No suggestion of robbery or sexual assault and the psychiatrists say that sado-masochism is unlikely judging from the position of the wounds. This joker just kills for the sake of killing and that's not a human motive.

"Two prostitutes, a bank clerk, a shop assistant and a dental nurse. Now this . . ." Pode looked at the body on the blood-stained carpet. Mary Blake (aged 45), deputy head mistress at a local primary school and a popular figure in the area. Miss Blake had taught the inspector's daughter and once again he felt deep personal loathing towards the man who had killed her.

"No common factor, no link between them; no rational motive. Nothing to give us a lead." Pode paused and considered his first thoughts when he had entered the room. *A slaughter house . . . savaged by an animal . . . Torn by a machine.*

"Savaged," he said aloud, turning to Rant who was writing in a notebook. "Can you describe the injuries to me, Doctor. The exact nature of her injuries?"

"Not precisely, Inspector, but here's a rough list."

"Thank you." The surgeon had held out the book and Pode frowned at his notes. "Lateral wounds inflicted by a heavy chopping weapon; a hatchet or a kitchen cleaver. Jagged incisions from a sharp-edged weapon; a knife or possibly a chisel. Oval incisions probably caused by a file or a marlin spike.

"But you believe that the actual murder instrument was that crucifix which crushed her skull?" Rant nodded and the inspector barked a gruff order to his sergeant. "The dates of the others, Clarke. The days on which they were found."

"Of course, sir." The sergeant opened a folder and flicked through the sheets of typescript. "Polly Mather, April the sixth. Norah Swain, May the fifteenth. Helen Landscombe, November the first . . ."

"That's enough." The *Nativity* bells seemed to be growing louder and Pode flopped down on his knees, though not to pray. The dates had rung a much clearer bell and he knew that there was a connection.

"The Vicar poses as a Christian priest," he said. "The Vicar also observes the Christian festivals and we've been blind fools.

"April the sixth; Easter Day. May the fifteenth; the Day of the Ascension. November the first; All Saints' Day. December the twenty-fifth; the day of Christ's birth.

"This joker has a motive all right. A sad, crazy motive, but there's method in his madness and he didn't slash and stab his victims haphazardly." Pode held a magnifying-glass over a gash in the dead woman's throat. "Do you believe in diabolical possession,

Doctor? Do you consider that a human being can be infected by the lusts of an animal, Sergeant Clarke? Blood lusts?

"I do and I'm looking at the evidence." The inspector motioned his team to join him. "A man kills six women to insult God, but man-made weapons did not kill them." He pointed at the gaping throat wound. "The cut of a knife? The slash of a hatchet.

"Red herrings, Doctor. Smoke screens, Sergeant Clarke. Distortions to obliterate traces of his real instruments, Constable Glossop. This cut isn't clean. There are perforations along both edges." His lens travelled to another rent at the side of the neck. "The axe blade has bitten deeply, but other bites are visible.

"The Vicar may kill at random, but he covers up his marks afterwards. Look at his marks, Constable. The marks of the Vicar . . . The mark of the . . .

"I told you to look, son." The young man had closed his eyes, and Pode repeated the order. "Look closely and pray that you'll never see such marks again.

"The marks of possession . . . The Mark of the Beast."

Detective Constable Glossop was impressed by Pode's statement. Chief Constable Brady was not.

"George Pode's getting past it," Brady said to the Superintendent (Crime) when the theory was discussed at a meeting.

"George is a fanciful fool," said the superintendent and a visiting commander from Scotland Yard agreed.

"Get the fool off the case and keep him quiet," the visitor advised. "A human beast who wears clothes! Who has teeth and nails which tear flesh and gnaw bone.

"Yes, get the fool off the case and make sure he keeps his own teeth closed. These murders have caused enough unfounded rumours without your Inspector Pode pouring oil on the flames.

"The public will be seeing Count Dracula or fanged Martians on their doorstep if Pode talks to the papers. Transfer the fool to another division."

"Quite right, Commander." The superintendent signified his agreement by thumping the conference table. "We'll catch the Vicar without any holy water, clairvoyants or crystal balls.

"Certainly without Georgie Pode and he's off the case as from now." He scribbled a memo to that effect.

"A man-beast with claws and fangs. Hobgoblins and demons, and bats in the belfry. George is batty himself . . . He's slipping . . . He's a superstitious has-been."

Logical conclusions, but logic didn't lead to the arrest of Mary Blake's murderer; nothing did. The Vicar died in bed and a long time elapsed before the superstitious fool was proved right.

How many other people shared Miss Blake's gruesome end? No one could say for sure; the figures were never verified.

Who or what killed them? A man with an animal's strength? A beast with human weapons? No one could be certain, and the point was academic.

The real question concerned Unity, but no one considered that till the case was officially closed. No one suspected that the Vicar had followers . . . Successors.

George Pode might have thought of an appropriate quotation, but if he had voiced it, who would have listened?

"My name is Legion; For We are Many."

One

(*Narrative of William Easter*)

I'd suspected that Mr Allen K. Smeaton was a bastard from the moment I was ushered into his office. It took me six months to realize I was right.

Mr Smeaton was a banker; the manager of the National Central's branch at Feltonford. A small, unimportant branch and a small, unimportant man. Allen Smeaton had an air of smug self-satisfaction, there was a Rotary pin in the lapel of his dark blue suit, and a tie around his neck denoted that he'd been semi-educated at a minor public school. I later learned that he was a churchwarden, a local councillor and chairman of the Feltonford magistrates' court. A self-righteous individual, though I must admit he was civil enough at first.

So, he damn well should have been. I and my common law wife Peggy Tey (the term common applies to Peg in the social as well as the legal sense of the term) wished to open an account at Smeaton's branch, and why not? The *Nat Cent* had recently announced that they would welcome customers with five pounds to place in their charge. We had three thousand times that amount . . . in cash.

"Yes, fifteen thousand pounds, Mr Easter." Smeaton had flicked through the notes to check my arithmetic and also to see that none of serial numbers tallied. The National Central might welcome small depositors, but they didn't want a stack of forgeries in their vaults. "Not a fortune these days, but a nest egg . . . a very nice nest egg.

"I'm surprised that you should have risked carrying such a sum around with you." He clicked his false teeth in concern for our safety, but he need not have worried. Mrs Peggy Tey was once a female wrestler in a night club, and Billy Easter can look after himself. There was a little knife I used to call Bloody Mary in my hip pocket and she'd defended her master on several occasions.

"A nest egg, an umbrella for a rainy day. May I ask what your profession is, sir?" He squinted at a couple of twenties while popping the question and I told him that I was a retailer of disposable ladies' underwear. There's no harm in asking, but getting a correct answer is a different matter. In that instance, however, my reply was true.

"Ah, a profitable line of business I imagine, and I hear you've taken a house on Cleveland Avenue. A most pleasant road and I hope you'll both be very happy in our little community. Feltonford is a friendly town. We pride ourselves on being good neighbours.

"Now, if you'll excuse me just a moment, I'll instruct my clerk to prepare the necessary forms." The suspicious sod could have given his instructions on the intercom, but he smirked and left the room and I knew why. Allen Smeaton had made a mental note of some of the numbers and he wanted to be sure they weren't on the police list. That the money had not been illegally acquired as they say.

He needn't have troubled. There was nothing wrong with the money, and I'd seen Sam Cohen draw it out of his own bank in the City; all shipshape and kosher. Sam may be a crook, but like most Jews he sticks to a bargain and pays cash on the nail. What he'd paid the cash for was no business of Mr Allen K. Smeaton's.

"Here we are, and if you'll both sign these documents." He bustled back and laid two forms on the desk. One would have been enough, but Peggy's a distrustful bitch and had insisted that the account be in our joint names.

"Thank you, Madam . . . Thank you, Sir. All is in order and once again may I bid you welcome to Feltonford. I live a few miles out of town myself, but you'll find we're a friendly neighbourhood. Strong community spirit and I'm sure you'll fit into our little community." Now that he knew the money wasn't forged, stolen or strayed our obliging bank manager became positively affable. An affability which increased when he recognized my own tie. "Ah, I see that you are an Oxford man, Mr Easter."

"Yes." Another truthful answer. I had been to Oxford, though I got booted out before the end of my second year. The original charges were Fraud and Gross Immorality, but the authorities altered them to idleness to spare my parents' feelings. They needn't have bothered. I've never cared for either of my parents and would have much preferred the first offences. Bill Easter may enjoy the odd tumble in the hay. He may be dishonest, but he's not idle. He's extremely hardworking and God what work I've done.

Bodyguard to a Dago dictator in South America at the age of twenty-one. Unfortunately the fool got himself assassinated a year later, though through no fault of mine.

Smuggler, gun-runner and bodyguard again. This time to Bruno Kremer, about the toughest gangster in East London. Like the Dago, Bruno got himself killed and for that I accept full responsibility. He received a bullet in the belly and I put it there.

I had also started a revolution in Africa once, where I got lumbered with Mrs Margaret Tey and lumbered is the operative word. Peggy is a hulking redhead who tops the scales at fifteen stone; a heavy cross for any man to bear.

My most recent venture was in antiques and it had profited up to a point. I'd managed to obtain an example of Renaissance goldsmith's art from a museum in Kensington. Catalogues and text books described the object as priceless, but Sam Cohen knew how I'd obtained it and the price was adjusted accordingly. As I've said, most Jews are honest. They drive a hard bargain, but they stick to the letter of the law. An agreement is an agreement . . . An Israelite's word is his bond. Sammy did drive a hard bargain. He paid up like the good scout he was.

Priceless object! The miserly devil only gave me fifteen.

Fifteen *thousand* of course. A fraction of what the thing was worth, though as Smeaton had remarked an umbrella; a nice nest egg. He'd been as pally as his type can ever be, but that was some months ago and the rains had come and our egg had vanished. I'd wanted a car, the landlord wanted his rent. The rates people, the gas and electricity people, the shopkeepers all demanded payment, and there was nothing to pay 'em with. Worst of all our business had failed to prosper. In under half a year we were in hock, but apparently there was no cause for alarm. Mr Allen K Smeaton and the National Central Bank were most helpful . . . most understanding and obliging.

Too obliging! I suppose I should have realized that there was a motive for such tolerance and generosity, but I didn't. I wasn't in the least surprised to receive a summons to visit Smeaton's office and I obeyed. Debts must be settled and creditors staved off, because *Mother Tey's Disposable Underwear* had failed to prosper.

MODERN LADIES GIVE THEIR KNICKERS TO THE DUSTMAN. I'd thought that that was a rather catchy advertising slogan, but the modern ladies hadn't shared my view. A warehouse was full of unsold tissues and we were bust. As I drove to the bank I wondered why Mr A.K.S. had let me overdraw in the first place. It took some time to find out.

"Please sit down and make yourself comfortable, sir." He waved me to a chair and produced a cigarette case. "Ah, you do smoke, Mr Easter." I'd accepted a fag and he leaned forward and lit for me. "Pleasant weather. A trifle humid perhaps, but one mustn't grumble." For an impatient usurer his manner was strange. Just as pally as on our first meeting, but . . .

Ingratiating might be the correct description and he was also ill-at-ease and looked far from well. There were bags under his eyes, his forehead was mottled with sweat and he'd lost weight.

"Yes, the atmosphere is extremely close, but I mustn't waste your time with idle chatter, sir." He had lit a cigarette himself and inhaled deeply. "I'm sure you know the state of your affairs, but let's see the exact figures." There was a plastic contraption on his deck and he leaned forward and pressed a row of buttons.

The thing had a screen which gleamed like a black-and-white television and showed our names with a line of numerals beside 'em. The line which shocked me because I hadn't realized our overdraft was quite so high.

"Over nineteen hundred pounds, Mr Easter." Smeaton mopped his brow with a handkerchief. "Not a serious deficit, but I gather you have no securities and your garment venture may soon be facing liquidation.

"Also that the house on Cleveland Avenue is only rented on a short-term agreement." He spoke as I'd expected him to speak, but not in the manner I expected. Though Mr Smeaton had the whip hand he appeared more saddened than angered by my predicament. Maybe the poor booby and his minions had failed to notice the debt and he'd get a rocket from head office. Perhaps he imagined I might have a rich aunt who'd square up before the inspectors called.

"But there's no need to panic. We all get into the doldrums now and again, and I'm sure a man with your attainments can easily change D.R. to C.R." He produced a notebook from his drawer.

"Attainments . . . Very considerable attainments, Mr Easter." He opened the book and donned a pair of spectacles. "I told you we're a friendly little community here and Dai Evans, the local police inspector, is a close friend of mine and a fellow Rotarian.

"Do you know Dai by the way, Mr Easter?" I shook my head and he smiled faintly. A curious sort of smile and I began to think that Allen K. Smeaton was a bit of a dark horse. "A pity because Dai knows a great deal about you and he was able to give me an outline of your rather adventurous career." The little smile widened as he saw me wince. "Please don't be alarmed, sir. Dai

Evans spoke in strict confidence and I naturally expect that you treat what I am about to say with equal discretion."

I bowed and assured him that I was the soul of discretion, whilst mentally condemning his pal, Inspector Lewis, to hell fire. *A strong sense of neighbourliness* indeed. The inhabitants of Feltonford obviously prided themselves on prying into their neighbours' affairs and Mr bloody Dai Lewis could go and jump off Snowdon. The police had nothing against me . . . not at the moment, and I was about to tell Smeaton so, and then changed my mind.

I might not be worried about the law, but I was dead scared of the unlawful. Only that morning I'd written a cheque for two hundred pounds to a pal of my own, and the pal had a bad temper. If that cheque bounced or Smeaton closed the account, Peg and I would have to get out of Feltonford fast. My best hope was to put on a brave face, promise him that my financial doldrums would soon be over and he could rely on the word of an Oxford man.

"But of course I rely on your word, Mr Easter, and I have no intention of pestering you with minor problems." He turned off the television apparatus and thumbed through his notebook.

"One thousand nine hundred and seventy three and a few odd pennies, sir, and we can forget that right away." He pressed a bell switch and a lugubrious female appeared. "Credit this to our customer's account, Miss Chaucer, and let me know the balance."

"Thank you, Miss Chaucer." The poet's namesake hurried away with a thick buff envelope in her hand and Smeaton dragged at his cigarette. The kind of drag which made me think of a spy's last favour before the firing squad.

"An anonymous benefactor has come to your rescue, Mr Easter, and your obligations will shortly be settled."

"What does the benefactor want in return, Mr Smeaton?" I knew who the anonymous Good Samaritan was of course. The obliging bank manager had rescued his debtor, but why? His chatty police inspector must have said that I had a criminal history, so one could rule out Christian charity. Mr Allen Karslake Smeaton might be a church warden, but I felt sure he was a bit short where the milk of human kindness was concerned. Why had he told the Chaucer girl to credit my account? Why should a pillar of *our little community* rush to the rescue of an improvident sinner?

"I need your expertise and knowledge, Mr Easter." He switched on the screen again and I saw that our account had a small balance. "I have paid you two thousand pounds as a retainer, sir, and there will be much more in return for your services." He leaned back and fingered his inferior old school tie and I noticed that two little nervous tics were trembling beneath his eyes.

"Yes, I need you, Mr Easter. I've needed you for some time, which is why I allowed you to overdraw, but there is no time left now and I must put my cards on the table." He stared at sunlight streaming through the window and his nervous twitches became more pronounced.

"As you know the weather has been abnormally hot and sultry and time is running out." In spite of the heat he shivered. "My poor lady wife and I have a problem, sir. A terrible burden has been thrust upon our hands and I am asking you . . . No, begging you to release us from it." He shivered again and his voice was so low that I could hardly hear him.

"We have to get rid of a very heavy . . . very dead . . . human body."

Dispose of a human body! Just like that, but whose body?

My first thought was that Mr Smeaton had killed someone. Possibly a female clerk whom he'd put in the family way. Maybe a bank inspector. Perhaps a rival for the headship of the Rotary Club, whatever that position is called.

If so, he could count me out as an accessory to murder and count himself in as a victim for blackmail. I wasn't going to face any murder charge, and I've never considered blackmail to be as despicable a crime as many people think. If you've done something which can land you behind bars it's better to pay up than be locked up, and I told Smeaton so loud and clear.

"Murder, Mr Easter! Do I look as though I am capable of murder?" As a matter of fact he didn't, but after making the accusation I held my peace and waited for further details. They were not forthcoming in the office, though he assured me his stiff had passed away from natural causes and the good name of his *lady wife* and himself were at stake. Important factors in *our little community*, and I'd understand the position as soon as I'd examined the cadaver. All most unfortunate—most embarrassing and distressing, but if I could spare an hour.

An hour for a man who'd just paid me two thousand quid! I could spare him the whole day, and he rang for Miss Chaucer and told her he was taking me out to lunch. I don't know whether she believed him, because until a few minutes ago I couldn't have been described as a particularly valued or lunch-worthy customer, but that's neither here or there. We left the bank, climbed into his car and set off to visit the dear departed.

Allen K. Smeaton was a nervous driver and he didn't talk much during the journey. He concentrated on the hazards of the route. I concentrated on the problems he had set me.

There are several ways to get rid of a human corpse, if you have the courage, the equipment and, most important of all, the solitude. The equipment Bruno favoured was a concrete mixer and four of his victims are now propping up the Inner London Motorway.

Failing concrete, you can use fire, acid, conventional burial or sling the body into the sea; suitably weighted. I've heard that animals can also be helpful; pigs in particular. A hungry porker will consume every scrap of edible tissue; bones included. Teeth are difficult to digest however, and get passed out through the bowels.

Yes, several ways, but we possessed no industrial furnace, no acid bath, concrete mixer or herd of swine. That left the sea or Mother Earth and they were definitely out. August . . . holiday time and the beaches crowded with trippers. A stifling month and the ground baked as hard as Bruno's motorway. We'd need a road drill to scoop a grave for Smeaton's stiff unless it happened to be a small child or a midget.

"Child . . . Midget!" I must have spoken aloud and Smeaton clicked his teeth sadly. "Henry Oliver was a huge man. Grossly overweight . . . Twenty-five stone at least and neither my wife nor I could move him.

"However I'm sure I can rely on you, Mr Easter. Dai Evans outlined your career, and you won't find me ungenerous. Two thousand pounds already, and there'll be another eight as soon as . . ." He drew up at a red traffic signal and groaned.

"You can't imagine the hell I've been through. The shame and disgrace . . . The vicar and the church council . . . The customers and head office." The lights had changed to green and he released the clutch pedal and we bucketed forward. "Ruin and crucifixion unless you can get rid of that vile man.

"Ten thousand is all I can raise at the moment, Mr Easter." There were tears, actual tears in his eyes as he listened to my question. "I'll try to find more later on, but I'm appealing to your charity . . . your common humanity now.

"The shame of it . . . My position in the community at stake . . . To be crucified and pilloried unless . . ."

Unless I could dispose of the defunct Henry Oliver for him. Ten thou' isn't much for saving a man from the cross or the pillory, but I promised to do my best and to hell with the vicar and head office, the customers and his fellow Rotarians. I'd no idea what the manager of a small bank earns, but Smeaton explained that he had three married children and was helping to pay off their mortgages. Also that his wife was undergoing psychiatric treatment in a private clinic. Ten thousand was probably the most he could stump up at short notice, and though I had no fondness for Mr Allen Smeaton I felt slightly sorry for him. I promised to shift his bulbous corpse even if we needed a block and tackle for the operation. I did, however, make it clear that if there was the slightest suspicion of foul play, I'd pay the garrulous inspector Evans a visit.

"Yes, foul, Mr Easter. *Foul* is the only description, though not in the criminal sense of the word. Henry Oliver was foul. Never suspected just how foul . . . how disgusting. Never dreamed what was going on till my dear wife . . ." He groaned still more abjectly and turned into the drive of his house.

A valuable house . . . A desirable property, as estate agents say, but I didn't desire it. The building dated from between the wars and was obviously soundly constructed and well-maintained. Three storeys, not including a basement. On the surface there was nothing amiss with Allen Smeaton's mansion, but I suddenly hated it. The house was a hostile house and as cheerless as a prison; though the paintwork was a cheerful pastel blue. For no reason I thought of exercise yards and strutting warders. Of cells and stale bread and governor's inspections. Of shackles, balls and chains and strait-jackets.

My reactions were mainly emotional, but there was a practical motive for my dislike of *Chez Smeaton*. The place provided no cover to remove Oliver's carcase.

The grounds were expansive, but they lay in a dip beside a road junction and possessed not a single tree nor a screening wall to conceal our activities. Every square yard was visible to passing motorists. Smeaton's house was not only a bad house, it was damned inconvenient.

"Please come this way, Mr Easter." We had left the car and while following him to the front door I noticed that the basement windows were tightly curtained. "You'll inspect the . . . remains in a moment, but first let me offer liquid refreshment." He led the way through a corridor and into a chintzy sitting-room which smelled of furniture polish, roses, carnations and another sweet smell which I didn't recognize, but felt I should.

"Help yourself to whatever you fancy. We've got most of the usual beverages, but I suggest that rum might be the best tonic under the circumstances." His trembling hand pointed at a sideboard, but I ignored the advice and poured out a large Scotch. I've never developed a taste for rum, though it is an excellent pick-me-up. Makes sailors fighting mad and is the only form of booze that actually increases the sexual powers. That's fair enough providing both partners to the union have had a skinful. The pong of the stuff would deter a satyr and turn a nympho frigid.

"Cheers, Mr Smeaton." He had mixed himself a small gin and tonic and I raised my glass and toasted him, "Now, you told me that time is important, so let's get on with the business. *On with the motley. Lead me to the wictim.*"

I thought the quotations were amusing, but Smeaton either lacked a sense of humour or was unfamiliar with opera or Charles Dickens. His expression remained abject and he pointed at the sitting-room door which we'd left open.

"Henry Oliver's there . . . down there. We couldn't remove him." His tremulous fingers showed me that there was another door across the passage. A heavy oak door which was slightly ajar, because the lock was broken.

"Yes, Cynthia, my poor dear lady wife had to shatter it with a hammer and chisel and he's still in the basement. You'll be able to examine him at your leisure, Mr Easter, but I'd have another whisky if I was you. Not a pleasant sight, I'm afraid . . . Extremely distasteful."

"I am not you, Mr Smeaton, and I've seen a lot of stiffs in my life; some of them decomposing." Though I'd recognized the third odour I laid aside my glass and walked into the corridor. "Come and show me the way." I'd naturally presumed he'd accompany me, but the craven bastard shrunk back and stammered.

"No . . . Can't face it . . . Vile . . . ho-rrible. My wi-fe. Cynthia . . . Nerv-ous break-down . . . Found her ra-aving.

"Please Mis-Mister Easter. Please pleas-se go alone. I'll pay you . . . pay you well, but don . . . don't ask me to lo-look at him."

"Very well, Mr Smeaton, but your poltroonery has just cost you another thousand pounds, bringing the total to eleven. Is that agreed?" He nodded and I opened the door, found a light switch at the top of the stairs and went down to have a squint at Pal Oliver.

The late and unlamented Harry Oliver couldn't harm me. He couldn't harm a fly, though the flies had probably been at work on him. Oliver was dead and his twenty-five stone were rotting. I felt no neurotic anxieties as I moved towards his pungent tomb, though I held a handkerchief over my nose and mouth for obvious reasons.

I had only one anxiety and it was purely practical. How was I going to dispose of his vast cadaver, but I'd cross that bridge when I came to it. Money, like love, usually finds a way and Bill Easter is not daunted by technical difficulties. Not when eleven thousand quid is involved, and lots more in the offing. Mr William Easter intended to put the squeeze on Mr Allen Karslake Smeaton for a long, long time.

I seem to think that Mr Easter hummed *Rock of Ages* as he walked down the stairs to the basement, but I can't be sure. I know that he saw the switch at the top of the stairs had activated another lamp in the basement. He could see it glimmering through a glass panelled door in front of him.

I know that Mr Easter felt completely self-confident as he approached the glass door, but I'm not sure what happened when he peered through one of the panels.

No, not sure. Not certain at all, but I suspect that my head must have jerked back and collided with the wall. I can't say whether it was the blow or the mental shock that stunned me.

The corpse of Henry Oliver was not responsible for my indisposition. Oliver was as dead as dead can be, though all I saw of him was one large, hairy leg protruding from a pile of blankets. It was the room itself which horrified me and after I'd regained my senses I beat a hasty retreat.

If Smeaton had not murdered Oliver, I'd wondered why he couldn't have sent for the undertaker or an ambulance to remove his unwelcome stiff . . . I knew. If Oliver had died of natural causes I wondered why my help was required . . . I knew.

I knew what the Vicar, the Rotary Club and all the rest of *Our Little Community* would have to say about Mr Allen K. Smeaton and his *Lady Wife*, and I said it myself after I returned to the sitting-room. Said it with feeling. "Pig," I shouted. "You filthy, unspeakable, bloody-minded pig."

Two

According to Allen Smeaton, it wasn't his fault and after my indignation abated I felt sympathetic. No sane man or his wife would have lived above that basement and if the conditions became public he'd have been ostracized, ridiculed and lost customers. The Smeatons were panic-stricken dupes. The pig was Oliver.

When their children married, the Smeatons decided to let the basement to a respectable single gentleman. They advertised in the newspapers and the first applicant was Henry Oliver. He had no current reference, having been abroad for some time, but appeared eminently respectable. He didn't quibble about the rent and all he required was peace and privacy.

The premises had been converted into a self-contained unit for the Smeatons' daughters before they left home and had its own bathroom, front door and telephone. Henry Oliver was satisfied and moved in. He hardly ever moved out.

A model tenant, but a tenant who could have ruined Smeaton's reputation if the authorities knew about his activities. The rent was popped through the letterbox on the first day of each month. He ordered his requirements by telephone. He occasionally asked the Smeatons to post a letter for him. Letters which appeared to be settlements of bills.

An excellent lodger, apart from one thing. Henry Oliver brought a lot of traffic to the house, though it didn't bother the Smeatons too much. Delivery vans kept arriving at frequent intervals. They left packing-cases for the lodger's collection. Smeaton and his missus didn't give the deliveries a thought till disaster fell, but before knocking my head against the wall I'd seen what those cases contained. Goodies . . . eatables and drinkables; nourishment.

I believe that there's a mental disease which leads to the hoarding of food and drink, and it's caused by anxiety. I've no idea what the name of the illness is, but Henry Oliver certainly suffered from it and I forced myself to go down the stairs again and have another squint.

Eatables! The flat resembled a tightly packed rubbish dump, though the rubbish must once have been extremely valuable. Chickens and joints of beef, crates of eggs, mutton chops, pats of butter and God knows how many empty and half-empty wine bottles. Old Harry Oliver had had enough provisions to keep a large family for a year, but they were all rancid, stale and putrid now. My first thought was why rats hadn't got at his hoard, but the answer seemed obvious. The place was too tightly packed for any rat to gain an entrance.

"The smell, Smeaton?" I had discarded the formal *Mister* on my return. "Surely you noticed the smell?"

"There was no smell, Mr Easter. No movement of air to bring the stench to the surface. Oliver kept his windows closed and he sealed them with tape. We didn't notice or suspect a thing till my lady wife . . ." He sighed abjectly and continued the story with his head in his hands.

Two months ago, Oliver had failed to put his rent through the letter-box. Nor did he answer the telephone or respond to a ring on his door bell. Smeaton was financially perturbed. His lady wife was motivated by charity.

A flu' virus had been raging at the time and Cynthia Smeaton became concerned for the tenant's welfare. While hubby was at his office, Florence Nightingale had decided to pay the invalid a visit. She had forced the staircase door with a hammer and chisel and gone down to take the poor man a mug of hot milk laced with whisky.

Milk! Whisky! My mind boggled. The poor man had had more milk and booze than an army of children and alcoholics could knock back, but Mrs S. didn't know that. She trotted dutifully along on her errand of mercy. She reached the glass door and . . .

"I found Cynthia in the hall, Mr Easter. She was beside herself with distress and horror. She was too ashamed to let me call for the local doctor. The dear girl was so loyal, so concerned for our reputation, and I shared her feelings when I looked into the flat myself." If Smeaton had had any hairs to tear he'd have torn 'em, but compromised by scratching his bald pate. "I had to get Cynthia to a nursing-home, of course. I drove her to London and she's still in that Harley Street clinic. A terrible expense, but she refuses to come home till the basement's been thoroughly cleared. Can you blame her?"

I couldn't blame her, but I wasn't a miracle worker and there were breakers ahead. Smeaton had hired me to dispose of a body. He had let our overdraft mount up after Oliver died and his matey police inspector outlined my history. He needed my help; you might say he'd almost blackmailed me, for my services. Fair enough; as long as he paid there were no hard feelings on that score and I was damn sure that he would pay.

But now he wanted his whole filthy basement cleared, which was a different matter, though I saw his point. The corpse itself weighed twenty-odd stone and between it and the front door lay several tons of garbage and polluted furniture. The material rubbish would have to be shifted as well as the human remains, and I hadn't bargained for that.

I hadn't a clue how the job could be done. I said that the deal was off and I helped myself to another Scotch while he pleaded and whimpered.

"Shut your mouth, Smeaton. Keep quiet and let me think." I was standing by the window finishing my drink when I cut him short, and stared out at the road. We had a load of garbage to dispose of and I suddenly realized the point of disposal.

It's strange how flashes of genius can be triggered off by commonplace events. Archimedes letting his bath overflow and leaping out with a cry of *Eureka* when he spotted that the volume of his body displaced an equal volume of water. The object which activated my genius was a cart. A dirty, dung-coloured vehicle crawling along the road with three dirty louts perched on the tail-board. Not a chariot for the gods, but I knew its destination. The words Feltonford Borough Council were printed on the side with a smaller inscription below them. *R.S. Potts, M.I.C.E., R.I.B.A., Borough Engineer.*

"You are a law-abiding citizen in many ways, Smeaton," I said. "You diddled the income tax authorities by not declaring Oliver's rent. You panicked and concealed his death, but I presume you pay your rates." He nodded abjectly and I raised my glass to toast Mr Potts.

"Good! Then we must see that you get value for your money." I smiled cheerfully and thought of our advertising slogan. *Modern ladies give their knickers to the dustman.*

With any luck, Henry Oliver and his hoard should be out of the house by morning.

Three

I'd decided on the disposal point, but getting our lumber there was a different matter, and as Smeaton had remarked, the hot weather made speed essential. A clock was striking two when he drove me back to the bank and I cashed a cheque for five hundred to cover expenses. There was no time to lose, but the Feltonford pubs don't close till three and I hurried across to the *Lamb and Flag* for female guidance.

Peggy was there as I'd expected, washing down a tasty meal of roast pork, dumplings and potatoes with a pint of draught Guinness. A repast which couldn't have done anything to improve her figure, but hadn't dulled her brain. Peg may not be very intelligent or educated, but she possesses a keen animal cunning and thinks quickly. She also possesses a large circle of acquaintance, and in ten minutes she had understood the position and selected our helpers.

Every small town has its handful of undesirables and Feltonford's bugbears were Michael and Robert Flood. Two brothers with records of petty crime and general delinquency. Peggy approached them, as they were said to be hard workers if one paid cash, and they were also the sons of Alderman Silas Flood, a prosperous haulage contractor.

"Do you want to earn a hundred quid for a night's work, Mike?" The brothers were in the billiards room and Peg came straight to the point.

"Yus."

"Do you mind working in really filthy conditions, Bob?"

"Noah."

"Can you borrow a ten-ton van with a winch and tail lift?"

"Yus."

The Floods were men of few words, but easy men to do business with. I handed over fifty pounds and outlined what was wanted.

The operation must take place in darkness for two reasons. No inquisitive motorist should view what was going on. Nor should Mike or Bob know where the rubbish came from. If they did know, they'd spread the news abroad and Smeaton's name would be mud in the community. Scorned and scoffed, cast out of the Rotary Club and the Church Council. The man who lived over garbage could never hold his head high again.

At eleven o'clock the Floods would procure the van from their father's yard and pick up Peggy outside the church. The van would then proceed to Smeaton's establishment with Peggy at the wheel and our labourers concealed in the back. In the meanwhile I would have gone Chez Smeaton by the last bus which left Feltonford at 9.45, to prepare the ground.

A prospect which horrified me, but it had to be done, and I could only see one minor snag. The disposal point was not open to the public till 7 a.m., and the van had to be returned to the yard before Father-dear-Father arrived at eight.

As Michael remarked, "The bloody swine will have our guts for garters if he finds we've borrowed the bitch." A tarnished cliché, but probably true, though I wouldn't waste any sympathy on the Floods. I gave 'em a list of a few other items I might require and we parted company. They to the billiards table, Peggy to the shops, I go to bed. I'd had an unnerving day and there was a horrible task in store for me.

I never realized how horrible.

It was Friday and Smeaton had lent me a key and arranged to spend the night in London and visit his stricken wife. The bus dropped me near his residence at ten sharp and I shouldered a rucksack and walked down the drive. All the curtains were drawn, and the house looked dead and even more sinister under the big August moon. It was sinister. It was a house of death, but I'd borrowed a couple of amphetamine tablets from Michael Flood, and felt as spry as a schoolboy on his way to the candy store. Candy store . . . Sweet shop! My elation decreased as I entered the sitting-room and thought of the rotting piles below my feet.

I hated the thought of visiting that basement, but Needs must when the Devil Drives. Mr Henry Oliver must be driven away to his resting-place and the Floods mustn't know what they were driving. Oliver had to be decently shrouded before the van arrived, though there was no question of my shifting his enormous corpse. That would be left to the labourers, but first things came first. I opened the bag and took out Peg's purchases. A tin of Jeyes Fluid, a pair of overalls, a breathing-mask and a roll of nylon cord. A slender cord, but immensely strong. It had to be strong to haul Oliver out of his hidey hole.

The mantelpiece clock was chiming the half-hour when I'd put on the overalls, donned the mask and started to move down the basement stairs. That left me forty-five minutes. Ample time to prepare the deceased before the Floods and Peggy came on the scene, but . . .

But I hadn't noticed that the ruddy glass door opened inwards and was jammed against a side of beef, a crate of eggs and a sack of potatoes. It took me a full ten minutes to break the panels and force an entry. I was glad that Peggy had included a case opener in her purchases; a useful item which I hadn't asked for.

I won't disgust you with the conditions in the flat, but another ten minutes must have passed before I clambered through the piled rubbish and reached the dear departed. When I did reach him I got a shock.

I think Smeaton had mentioned that his tenant had had a beard. I know I'd seen a hairy leg protruding through the blankets during my first visit, but after I pulled back the blankets, I almost vomited through the face mask. Not because of the stench of decomposing flesh; the mask and a dollop of Jeyes Fluid took care of that. Not because I was involved in a murder. Mr Oliver appeared to have died peacefully. It was the sight and the size of the man that caused my distress.

Mr Smeaton had estimated that Oliver weighed around twenty-five stone . . . he looked far heavier. Though the body was naked, he appeared to be fully dressed or wrapped in a travelling-rug. More minutes elapsed before I realized that the rug was hair. Thick, matted hair which covered him from head to toe. Human hair, but it didn't seem human. The light bulb was dim and for a moment I imagined that some vast, dead animal was lying on the bed before me.

But only for a moment. I didn't stop and examine Harry Oliver for long. Time was running out and I covered him up with his bedclothes, and got to work with the nylon. According to its manufacturers the cord had a breaking strain of over a ton, but what about the bed itself . . . what about the sheets and the blankets? Though I've got great faith in my God, I knew that he'd have to use all His powers to help me then, and I must have said a dozen prayers to Him while I swaddled Oliver up, looped the line and tied the knots.

Tight corners and tight knots. A dozen prayers and at least a dozen knots, but I was still far from confident that the shroud would hold. If Henry Oliver came apart in transit, the fat would be in the fire. Michael and Robert Flood could put the squeeze on me.

But there's no point in dwelling on future misadventures either, and in that instance there was no time to dwell, because the funeral party had arrived. I heard a diesel engine and groped my way to the front door. Fortunately there was a key in the lock and the jemmy was not required. When I opened the door I saw that Peggy had reversed the van into position and our helpers were preparing to start work.

"Right, Bob. Let's get cracking." Michael didn't appear to be shocked by the condition of Oliver's abode. "If there's nowt you want salvin, Mr Easter, we'll use the net and grapple."

I didn't want anything salvaged and a contraption of wire and hooks was dragged out of the van. The engine was started, a winch revolved, and the operation began.

As Robert remarked a few minutes later, there was to be no muckin' abaht. Every large object was attached to the hooks, the smaller articles were piled into the net and one by one the loads were hauled towards the tail lift with much creaking and groaning. Smeaton probably lost some valuable furniture, but most of the stuff was too contaminated to be touched by hand.

"Let the bleedin' wagon do the work," Michael said, as a Victorian wardrobe crashed up into the van, but he was too modest. The Flood Brothers worked like Trojans or rather like Blacks were once supposed to work. The Floods also showed a deal of intelligence. When the number of wine bottles was revealed, Michael slung them into a metal bath, which had been brought along for emergencies. Robert smashed them with a bricklayer's hammer, and several hundred flagons were reduced to two bathfuls. By midnight, the front room was almost cleared and Peggy and I saw that our serfs could be left to their own devices. The labourers were worthy of their hire. The hirers could relax.

We went to Smeaton's premises, helped ourselves to Smeaton's drinks and made ourselves comfortable. I changed out of the overalls, had a wash and brush-up and laid down on Smeaton's chintzy sofa, but I couldn't relax. The sounds below were disturbing. Our industrious assistants were cleansing Oliver's Augean stables, but what about Oliver himself? What if the hooks tore the blankets . . . what if the cords snapped? Stripping a flat was one thing . . . removing a body another. The Floods might be excellent servants, but I was damn sure they'd be harsh masters. If they discovered what those blankets concealed, a hundred pounds wouldn't satisfy them. They'd squeeze us for every penny Smeaton had promised and more. The brothers would take our eyes and call back for the sockets.

"Sorry, Mr Easter, but we've hit a snag." Dawn had started to break when Michael knocked on the front door and I felt that my fears were justified. They hadn't hit a snag. They'd discovered the body and we were in trouble. "You'd best come and look for yourself, sir. Everything's been shifted, but there's one lot that needs thinking about."

One lot . . . the lot that mattered. The hairy corpse of a large, dead man, and my hands shook as I followed Mike down to the basement.

A basement which was hardly recognizable as the hellhole I'd visited earlier. Almost every scrap of furniture and every morsel of putrid food had been removed. The floors had been swept and sprayed with Jeyes Fluid. Michael and Robert had done an excellent job and my spirits soared when I saw the snag.

Not the bed, nor its occupant. Henry Oliver was safely tucked away in his hearse, and the thing was a desk. A nice oak desk, though it was spattered with broken eggs and melted butter. I asked Mike what the problem was and received a doleful answer.

"You're paying us to clear out the whole place, sir, but I'm afraid we can't do it. That sod's too heavy for the winch and the clutch keeps slippin'. We might be able to break 'er up with an axe, but there ain't no time. Must have the lorry back in the yard before Dad gets there."

I was about to say to hell with the blasted desk, as long as the corpse was aboard, but checked myself. I looked at my watch, I looked at the sun coming up through the doorway and appeared disappointed. It was a pity they hadn't fulfilled their obligations, but I didn't want them to fall into Alderman Flood's bad books. "Leave the desk and make off while the going was good."

The brothers were clearly relieved. They collected their tackle and climbed into the rear of the van. Peggy drove and I sat beside her with a song in my heart.

The long night's task was done, the job was completed to my full satisfaction, and the morning's work should be as easy as falling off a log. With the help of Mr Potts, the Borough Engineer, a moron could dispose of Oliver's garbage and his huge, hairy carcase.

The disposal point was appropriately situated between a geriatrics' hospital and the crematorium and its services were available to the general public during the forenoon of every Monday, Wednesday and Saturday from the hours of 7 a.m. (Bank Holidays excluded). Gaining admission was a simple matter. A fellow with a face like an outraged turkey cock accepted a fifty pence gratuity with ill-grace and ordered Peggy to reverse up a slope. She did so inefficiently, and at the top of the ramp, Michael and Robert took over. Mike activated the tipping mechanism and the rear of the van tilted. Bobby stood by with a rake to see that nothing was left behind. Inch by inch the floor of the truck rose and its load started to slide. Down went Smeaton's furniture, down went Oliver's provisions, down went Oliver's body. Down onto a slab to join a pile of other discarded possessions. A pile which would soon be scooped up by a bulldozer stationed nearby with its engine running and blade at the ready.

"Rock-a-bye, Baby, on the ramp top. When the van tilts the cradle will drop." I hummed as I watched baby drop. Baby and cradle and baby's bottles, they all went down to the slab and the dozer blade shovelled them towards a concrete trench. A hydraulic ram which would squeeze Oliver and his unsavoury goods into a solid block not much larger than a television set or Mr Smeaton's overdraft scanner.

I caught a glimpse of one hairy arm as the blade sliced through the blankets, but no one else saw it. I hurried the Floods away, paid them off and we arranged to meet for a drink and celebrate our toil.

Why not? Celebrations were in order. Mr A. K. Smeaton would be duly grateful and express his gratitude as per agreement. The ailing Mrs Smeaton could return home. Mr Henry Oliver was at rest in the council's crusher.

Four

Smeaton returned to Feltonford during the afternoon and settled the score like a gentleman. He wasn't a gentleman, and I don't know how he managed to collect the money at such short notice. Maybe his lady wife had had an account in London, but that was not my business. The notes were there in his brief-case all present and correct and we locked them away and prepared to spend a week of relaxation.

I had no worries about Oliver. The municipal ram operated at a pressure of seven hundred pounds to the square inch and he had been well and truly dealt with. On the following Monday he and the other compressed rubbish would be loaded onto lorries and transported to a disused gravel pit near Oxford. We should have forgotten him.

The trouble is that curiosity kept rearing its head. I wanted to know more about the Smeatons' obnoxious tenant. I wanted to know what was inside the desk we'd left at the flat. By Wednesday, my impatience boiled over and I decided to pay Smeaton a call and ask whether he'd still got it. An unnecessary decision. Allen K. Smeaton had got the desk and he called on me.

The desk had been puzzling Mr Smeaton, too. He liked the damn thing, and his missus loved it. As soon as she had got home from the Harley Street asylum, she inspected the flat, she took a fancy to that desk and consulted an expert. One of Smeaton's Rotarian cronies who ran an antique shop and said it might be worth a packet providing the interior was in good nick. Mrs S. gave the exterior a polish and the wood came up a treat. Not oak as I'd imagined, but Bloodheart. A rare tree only found in the northern regions of South America and virtually extinct.

The desk was the single piece of furniture that Oliver had actually owned. The Smeatons had acquired some compensation for the trouble he'd caused them, but as usual there was a snag. The lid and the drawers were secured by two metal bars running down through the frame and the bars were locked. Without a key they couldn't open them, so would I oblige again?

I would, but I didn't express any willingness at first. Though I appreciated Smeaton's predicament, I doubted his veracity. If the desk was as valuable as his pal with the antique shop said, he could hardly let his lady wife knock it about with hammer and chisel as she'd done to the staircase door. But, as his pal was in the furniture business, surely he could recommend a locksmith? Allen Smeaton also suspected that there was something of interest inside Oliver's cabinet. He didn't want any local tradesman discovering what that something was.

"Please, Mr Easter. Please persuade him to help us, Mrs Tey." I had played hard to get and he appealed to Peggy with a winsome smile. "As a lady of taste you must know what a joy it is to own really lovely things, and I'd not be asking either of you to do anything illegal."

Quite true. The illegalities had taken place on the Friday and Saturday and almost everybody was happy. Smeaton's further remuneration had been paid into a Barclay's bank in London. Oliver was in his Oxford gravel pit.

Only the Flood brothers were unhappy. They'd celebrated our success in the Lamb and Flag and it proved to be their last visit. Bob had thrown a pint of beer over the landlord. The brothers were forbidden the pub for life and due to appear before the magistrates.

"Very well, Smeaton. We'll look at your desk, but I'm making no promises. I will however make you an offer." I paused to consider the situation and then stated my terms. Providing I could open his *objet d'art* without too much damage, the contents would be split in the following manner. Any easily realizable assets, such as money, stamps and jewellery to be divided equally between the Smeatons and ourselves. Any non-realizable items like private papers, correspondence or a diary to be ours.

A one-sided bargain if my suspicions were correct, but Smeaton accepted them quickly. A bit too quickly I thought at the time, but I may have been wrong. He was a bank manager and he considered that Oliver's desk contained articles which could be banked. I believed something rather different because Smeaton had told me quite a lot about his tenant. Henry Oliver had had no job and no bank account, yet he'd squandered money on food and drink and paid the Smeatons more than a hundred quid a week. Paid him in postal orders, so who had posted those orders? I was damn certain that Oliver had been blackmailing someone and I wanted to know who that someone was.

Probably blackmail had never crossed Smeaton's mind except as a subject of righteous indignation. "Contemptible swine . . . Parasites preying on human weakness . . . All got our little failings . . . hah-hah-hah. But to be subjected to torture by vultures . . . bacteria . . . Sewer rats who never show their faces."

Noble sentiments voiced by an ignoble man. Allen Karslake Smeaton had diddled the income tax by failing to declare Oliver's rent. He had committed a crime by foolishly concealing a death. He wasn't responsible for the death, of course. I was convinced that Oliver had died of overeating, overdrinking and lack of fresh air and exercise.

But he was still a crook and I could have blackmailed Mr Allen Smeaton when he mentioned the bun in his basement. I hadn't, but why couldn't the sanctimonious fool realize that parasites form a necessary part of society? Vultures consume offal and rats help to keep the drains flowing. Without bacteria enriching the soil we'd all starve to death. If I hadn't cleansed the Augean stables, Head Office, the Rotary Club and *our little community* would have slung Allen K. Smeaton to hell and Halifax.

Smeaton had forgotten a quotation. "Big fleas have little fleas upon their backs to bite 'em." I remembered the quote but I never considered just how big the big fleas might be.

What had Oliver nibbled at . . . Who did I hope to set my teeth into?

Peggy and I visited the Smeatons that evening and the flat was clean and odourless, except for a strong whiff of Jeyes Fluid. The curtains had been removed and sunlight glinted onto Oliver's desk which had been polished by the loving, though slightly tremulous hands of Cynthia Smeaton. A thing of beauty indeed . . . a possession to be envied.

I'm not a connoisseur, but I can recognize craftsmanship and first-class materials, and I saw that Smeaton's antique dealer was right. The sun gave the Bloodwood panels a fine purplish sheen and they were inlaid with what I imagined was bone or ivory. I praised da Lawd that I hadn't let the Floods rip 'em apart with an axe. The brasswork gleamed appealingly, though the locks had a sneering gleam as though challenging me to try to force them. A sacrilege which I had no intention of committing. My hands would be just as loving as Cynthia Smeaton's, though a lot steadier.

I promised to take Miss Bloodwood's virginity gently, which was a damn silly promise. Other people had opened that desk in the past, including the nauseous Oliver, but they'd had keys. Keys which were now in the Oxford gravel pit, and I had to make my own. Not a difficult task, but there are tricks to every trade and why should the Smeatons learn one of my trades? I'd insisted on solitude for the operation and a gentleman's agreement is an agreement even if it hasn't been drawn up by gentlemen. I jerked a thumb at the stairs and told 'em to leave us alone.

They went. Smeaton reluctantly, his lady wife with eagerness, probably imagining that the desk contained more of Oliver's tuck-shop horrors. Broken eggs, rotten meat and a few marrow bones for a rainy day. Peggy and I waited till we heard the upstairs door close behind them and then I started work.

We'd brought a set of blanks, some cobbler's wax and a file with us, but they weren't necessary. A boy scout armed with a length of stiff wire could have penetrated Miss Bloodwood's defences and wire was what I used.

A short length shaped like an 'L' moved the steel tumblers, the wards drew back and I thought we were home and dry. We should have been if Oliver hadn't kept his flat so foetid and musty. The locks opened easily, but I couldn't shift the metal rods securing the lid and the drawers. Both bars were corroded by moisture and set solid in their tubes.

Brutal methods were required and I apologized to Madame Bloodwood and produced a bottle and hypodermic syringe. I also told Peggy to open the door and the windows and stand well back. Spirits of salt can clean most non-ferrous metals. They can also do unpleasant things to the throat and lungs; especially in enclosed spaces. I held a handkerchief to my nose, filled the syringe and doused the channels.

"Give me a fag, Peggy." She had gone outside and I joined her and took a deep breath. Hydrobomic acid has a hell of a pong and the flat smelled almost as bad as it had been during Oliver's tenancy. Apart from cleansing metals, the stuff's also used by doctors as a depressive and I didn't want to be depressed. I felt elated and I wanted to stay that way. I somehow sensed that when we opened the desk we'd hit the jackpot and find a crock of gold.

Gold! Gold has always fascinated me and I thought about it while I dragged at the cigarette. A fascination shared by the majority of people though I don't know why. Perhaps my fascination is because gold is purely decorative. Maybe it's the weight or the sheen of the soft sensual texture. Possibly romantic associations and legends arouse my own romanticism. Fairy Gold . . . Rainbow's End and Eldorado . . . The City of the Great Gilded Man.

Whatever the cause, humanity has always craved for gold and I dreamed about it as we waited for the stench of acid to disperse. Pipe-dreams probably. If Henry Oliver had paid his rent in ducats or guineas I might have had reason to dream, but . . .

But . . . but. Hope springs eternal and the tiny word of hope kept ticking through my brain. Miss Bloodheart might not have any precious metal lodged in her guts but I somehow knew she would set us off on a treasure hunt and I started to hum a sea shanty.

"Beyond the Chagres River,
Men say, the story's old,
Lie paths which lead to mountains
Of purest virgin gold."

"Come on, Bill. It's safe enough now." Peg interrupted me before I started the second verse and I took a cautious sniff and walked back into the flat. The smell of gas had vanished, but the acid had marred Miss Bloodheart's beauty slightly, but done what we intended. The first handle twisted at a touch and I pulled the rod out smoothly. The second rod was slightly more stubborn, but a sharp wrench freed the bar and I laid them both aside. Mr Oliver's chest was ours to open, but I didn't raise the lid at once. I'd been dreaming of gold and I wanted those dreams to continue. I couldn't bear the thought of my hopes crumbling.

"I won't give a penny for your thoughts, Bill. I can read 'em like a book. You're scared, darling. You think there's a booby trap inside this thing, but I'm not scared. Cowardice isn't one of my failings."

Maybe funk wasn't one of Peg's failings, but lack of manners came high on the list and so did lack of imagination.

"Keep your fingers crossed, Billy-boy." She snorted and pushed me aside. "Here goes."

"Christ . . . Jesus Christ." She had grasped the edge of the lid and heaved it up. She snorted again and staggered back, reeling against me as though something had slammed her in the belly. She regained her balance and craned forward, thrusting her hands into the top compartment and fondling its contents. She wept for joy. "We've made it, darling," she said, pulling me against her ample breasts and delivering a slobbery kiss. "Money . . . Loads and loads of lovely money."

Money! We never discovered how much money Harry Oliver had kept in his desk. Ten . . . Twelve . . . fifteen thousand pounds perhaps. After about half an hour we stopped counting. Why waste time thumbing through trash? Oliver had acquired a considerable small fortune over the years, but it was mainly worthless apart from a few British postal orders. Stacks of peseta notes issued by the Bank of La Libertad, capital of the Republic of Nueva Leon in South America. The bank had gone out of business long ago. Nueva Leon had lost its independence.

I'd once visited Leon and often wondered why it had existed in the first place. A sprawling stretch of wilderness running along the banks of the Selva River. The population might have numbered a couple of million (most of them forest Indians) before the United Nations annexed the territory. The government was composed of a bunch of inefficient oligarchs who allowed the river to silt up and become impassable to shipping. In earlier days there was supposed to be a considerable source of precious metals and gem stones in the interior, but the mines had been worked out and the economy was based on the export of timber. With no ships able to collect the timber that export ceased and the republic became bankrupt. A series of revolutions and counter-coups raged for almost three years till the U.N. cried a halt. A peace-keeping force of Americans, British, West Germans and other nationalities landed. The oligarchs fled or were torn to pieces by their disgruntled subjects. I believe that the country was still governed by a sort of International Brigade, but that was no concern of mine. My emotions were sorrow. Not a banking house in the world would pay a penny for Oliver's hoard and the original Leonian currency was discredited. I'd dreamed of gold . . . I'd unearthed dross.

"There's always the postal orders, Bill." Peggy was still rummaging through the gaily engraved bills and had separated a few sheep from the goats. "I make it about eight hundred, but . . ." She suddenly stamped her foot like Rumplestiltskin in a rage, cursed loudly and held out one of the orders for my inspection.

"They've expired . . . They're all six months out of date and . . ."

"and equally useless, Peggy." I'd started to examine the drawers, but there appeared to be nothing of value and I told her to summon the Smeatons. Though the paper money was worthless I suddenly had a strange feeling about Mr Henry Oliver. I wanted to know a lot more about the basement's former occupant.

"Nine hundred and twenty pounds in postal orders and all expired. At least twenty thousand in Leonese pesetas and most international banks would have exchanged them a year and a half ago." Smeaton was a quick calculator, and the amount of the loss had almost reduced him to tears. "Why couldn't Oliver have asked my advice? Why didn't he deposit them with me before the new currency was issued? Why didn't he cash the orders before they expired? What use are they to anyone now?"

"They might come in handy if there's a strike in the toilet paper industry." Though I shared his disappointment I'd retained my sense of humour. "Now, stop whimpering and tell me what you know about Henry Oliver. All you know, Smeaton, from the moment he took the flat."

"Oliver came here eleven months ago, Mr Easter." Allen Smeaton was still checking his tenant's obsolete hoard, and Cynthia answered me; a small bird-like woman who might have been rather pretty, if her face wasn't so pale and haggard. "I wasn't at home when Allen interviewed him. We knew nothing about the man and Allen accepted his story about having been abroad and never asked for references.

"Oh, what fools men are, Mrs Tey." Mrs S. put the blame on her male partner and appealed to Peggy for support. "Why couldn't Allen have realized the man was incapable of handling his financial affairs? Why couldn't he have insisted on inspecting the premises from time to time? Why not chat to Oliver and ask about his livelihood? All our own furniture contaminated and destroyed! Only this wretched desk left to show for what I've suffered.

"No, the desk didn't come with him, Mrs Tey." She considered Peg's question and moved round to the back of the thing. "It was delivered several months later by a depository in Southampton. The place wasn't in such a state then, of course, but I remember how the men grumbled at the weight. It took four of them to move the desk in and Oliver just stood aside and didn't offer to help at all. They had an Alsatian dog in the van with them, and he was terrified, of course. His hands were shaking so badly that he could hardly sign the receipt.

"Here's the copy, Mr Easter." She pointed to a slip stuck on the rear panel and I knelt down and squinted at it. A notice stated that the desk had been deposited at a Southampton warehouse in June 1979 and kept in store for eighteen months.

The summer of 1979, roughly the time that the Leonian government had been given the heave-ho. Oliver must have been in Nueva Leon just before the U.N. stepped in. He had somehow acquired a great deal of money, but why hadn't he changed it while he could? Why let it lie in a warehouse till the notes were dishonoured? Even more curious was why he hadn't bothered to cash the postal orders.

I snatched a wad of orders out of Peg's hand and something seemed to strike me like a blow. The dates and the amounts varied, but there was one common factor. Every order had been issued from a post office in Scotland or the Outer Isles. Surely that should give us a clue to the person who had sent them?

"Henry Oliver was a recluse, Mr Easter." Smeaton interrupted my chain of thought. "I told you that he hardly ever left the premises and I think he was too frightened to venture out and cash the orders. All his supplies were delivered, as you know, and he gave me his letters to post. Poor man; even though he caused us so much distress, I suppose we should pity him."

"Poor man!" It was Cynthia's turn to deliver a Rumplestiltskin stamp on the floor boards. "Pity! How can you use such a heartless expression, Allen? Owing to your wanton stupidity I had to live over a monster. To nurture a viper in my bosom."

An unjust and inaccurate cliché. Even the smallest of vipers couldn't have found shelter between Cynthia Smeaton's skinny breasts, and I wouldn't have blamed hubby if he'd lost his temper and clouted her.

"Yes, it was my fault, Mr Easter. I should have suspected what Oliver's trouble was . . . why he became a recluse." Hubby closed his eyes for a moment to bring back memories. "When Henry Oliver came to see me, his first questions were whether we kept a dog or were ever likely to keep one. He also wanted to know whether there were any dogs nearby.

"We don't keep a dog, of course, and there weren't any dogs in the neighbourhood at the time. I was quite truthful, but some months after Oliver accepted the tenancy, Miss Lampton bought a couple of dachshunds. Friendly little beasts, but for some reason Oliver was terrified of them." Smeaton opened his eyelids and stared out of the window. "I remember the incident distinctly. Oliver was sitting in the garden when Mary Lampton's bitch, Sally, squeezed through the fence with the dog, Fred, behind her. They were only looking for rabbits or a squirrel, but when Henry Oliver noticed them . . .

"It's difficult to describe, Mr Easter. Oliver stood up, and I've never seen such abject terror on a human face and not only the face. His whole body seemed to shrivel and grow old in seconds and even though he was so heavily bearded I knew that his skin was as white as ivory. He looked as though he was about to run, and then changed his mind when he saw that Sally was wagging her tail and coming towards him. A friendly beast as I've said, but Henry Oliver crept back towards his door as though she was a fiend from hell. Made me think of a piece of poetry. Can't recall the exact words, but it's about a traveller who discovers a demon is after him."

"Coleridge . . . The Ancient Mariner." As it happened I did recall the verse and I felt a sneaking sympathy for Harry Oliver.

> "As one who on a lonely road does walk in fear and dread,
> And having once looked back, walks on and turns no more
> his head.
> Because he knows a fearful fiend does close behind him
> tread."

Many people dread certain animals and I mean *dread*; not are frightened by. You're naturally frightened if a lion or an angry bull comes charging at you, because they can do you physical harm. But a rat won't hurt you unless it's cornered or infected with bubonic plague. No European bats are dangerous and the bite of an adder is hardly ever lethal.

But as George Orwell made it clear in *1984*, some of us have an animal horror which is quite irrational, but also unbearable. Snakes and insects are the most usual . . . Rodents and birds are pretty common.

Terror of domestic pets is mercifully rare, unless you've been scratched by a cat or bitten by a dog during what psychiatrists call *the formative years* of your life. It is probably the worst phobia of all because the creatures are domestic. They want your company.

Suppose your own bugbears are spiders or rodents. Try to imagine your feelings if an affectionate tarantula was sunning itself on every street corner hoping to be stroked or rub its side against you. What would it be like if whenever you entered a public house a gigantic sewer rat rose from the hearth to nuzzle your hand?

Henry Oliver hadn't seen Miss Lampton's friendly little Sally and Fred squeeze through the fence. He had seen two fiends out of hell and reacted accordingly.

Canophobia; a sad, pathetic and tragic disease. Difficult for me to understand, because by and large I like dogs and I know how to deal with 'em.

However my own attitude towards our canine chums was neither here nor there, and neither was Henry Oliver's, as I thought in my ignorance. I wanted to know the origin of his dud notes and outdated postal orders and when Smeaton stooped and opened the last drawer I cried halt.

Allen Smeaton had agreed that any non-negotiable assets should be our property and under the usual litter of worthless paper money I saw some items held together by a rubber band. Items which might prove negotiable, though only in the right hands. I pulled them out of his ignorant hands and had a squint.

Item One: a page from the London *Daily Globe*. *Item Two*: a passport with a slice of bacon wedged between its centre like a bookmark. *Item Three*: an egg-stained notebook or a diary.

I didn't bother to examine the passport or the little book immediately. It was the newspaper that had attracted my attention. I thought I'd recognized a picture on the crumpled paper and when I'd released the band I imitated the Smeatons' petulant stamps and cursed.

Allen Smeaton had paid me ten thousand pounds to dispose of his tenant and even after deducting the Floods' remuneration you might say that that was a fair fee for a night's work.

If so, you'd be wrong and after I opened the passport I cursed again. I cursed Peggy. I cursed Michael and Robert Flood. I cursed Mr Potts, the borough engineer, and his hydraulic crusher. Worst of all I cursed myself.

I had been dreaming of gold and I'd destroyed a treasure. My haste to get rid of Henry Oliver had cost us a fortune. Henry Oliver had never existed, but he'd been worth a packet before his carcase was compressed into a cube and tossed down the Oxford gravel pit. Henry Oliver's real name was the Rev. Oliver Hendricks and he'd been a bad boy. The police, three newspapers, a group of wealthy philanthropists and the government wanted to know the whereabouts of Canon Hendricks.

A very bad and extremely valuable boy. There was a reward of a hundred thousand pounds to the person who located him.

Five

The Savage . . . The Bent Vicar. Peggy and I had left the Smeatons with their desk and their dud notes and postal orders and returned to our rented house. Left 'em in ignorance and taken the three items which might be of value to us.

I stress the word *might*. No one would pay a reward for Henry Oliver or Oliver Hendricks now, but somebody had sent him those orders. Somebody who could be an accessory to murder.

There was no doubt that Hendricks had been a multiple killer. The Vicar had hit the headlines for several months and his career had reaped a rich harvest. The Press stated that at least ten women had died under the Vicar's knife, hatchet and chisel. His diary suggested the total was higher.

"Easter Day—Polly Mather. Cloudy night and raining.

"May the 15th. The Ascension. Did not know her name, but raddled hag . . . Horrible.

"Christmas Eve. Mary Blake . . . A nice woman. May God forgive me."

Peggy had telephoned a pal on Fleet Street and I checked the diary against what he'd told her. "Good Friday . . . Ellen Yeats; Dental nurse. Why do I mock Christ and destroy his creations?"

Prostitutes were the killer's first victims, but he soon spread his net wider. Every type and class of woman seemed to have aroused the wrath of the vicar.

His wrath, but not his lust apparently. Peg's friend confirmed that there was no suggestion of sexual assault in any of the cases, and robbery was definitely not the motivation.

The Vicar savaged women because he hated women and he

demonstrated his hatred with a variety of weapons. Each body had been hacked and slashed after death and some of the corpses were barely recognizable.

The police were baffled . . . The public infuriated. The hundred thousand pounds reward I mentioned was raised and offered for the Vicar, but no one suspected Canon Oliver Hendricks. Not until he attacked his second married woman. His last victim . . . the one who got away.

Mrs Gladwys Cronin was divorced and lived alone in the Scottish town of Stirling. Alone apart from a dog; an aged and almost toothless character who answered to Rusty. The assault took place on June the 3rd (Whit Sunday). Gladwys was in her sitting-room reading a newspaper. Rusty was in the garden doing his business. The back door was open, the Vicar knocked on the front.

"*CANINE HERO . . . RUSTY TO THE RESCUE.*" I seem to remember that one headline was printed in scarlet. I distinctly recall a series of television eulogies featuring the event.

"I owe me life to old Rust." The screen had shown a vacant-faced woman sitting on a sofa with a disagreeable spaniel at her side. "Nothing's too good for Rust now, and he'll get double helping of Smith's Prime Chunks for the rest of his days."

Doubtless Mrs Cronin got well paid by Messrs Smith for advertising their product. Doubtless Rusty's days were shortened by gorging his double helpings, but the sale of Prime Chunks rose considerably.

"Just sittin' there I was. Readin' *The Globe* when I heard a knock on the door, so I got up and looked through the glass," Mrs Cronin had told the interviewer. "There was a clergyman on the step, but I didn't suspect a thing, so I . . ."

So the stupid cow opened the door and the clergyman came in. The clergyman smiled and Gladwys Cronin came to her senses and remembered the Bent Vicar. "I was petrified. I couldn't even scream, let alone run. I just stood there, all of a tremble, waiting for the fiend to slice me and then . . ."

And then Rusty had returned from the garden and it was the fiend's turn to tremble. He had shuddered and staggered back when he saw the dog. To use Mrs Cronin's own words: "He looked as though a mug of acid had been tossed in his face." He had bolted through the door as Rusty growled and bared his decayed fangs.

The police hadn't believed that the killer was an actual cleric. They imagined they were dealing with an impersonator who got a kick from dressing up in clerical attire as well as other aberrations. They made identi-kit sketches and showed 'em to Mrs Cronin and other witnesses, but that didn't help the rozzers for a while. The case remained unsolved till some one compared the likenesses to a photograph in an old parish magazine and recognized the Vicar. Canon Oliver Hendricks, Rector of All Saints, Sodbury-on-Thames, was clean-shaven but his eyes and ears gave him away and the hunt was on.

The Canon had deserted his flock sometime before the killings began. He had received a call to spread the Gospel in foreign lands and departed to South America. The emigration records showed that he had returned to England in good time to commit the first murder however. They did not show where he had been after landing at Southampton.

But the bent Vicar attacked no more women following Rusty's intervention. The Rev Oliver Hendricks was presumed to have taken his own life in a fit of remorse. Mr Henry Oliver took Smeaton's flat. The tumult and the shouting died, but the reward remained.

"A reward which we'll never be able to claim, Bill." Peggy was leaning over my shoulder. "A hundred thousand smackers slung into the crusher and flushed down a drain." She gulped like a drain herself and then moved away from me and I saw her expression change. Her flabby features hardened like lava setting into granite and there was an eager gleam in her eyes. "We can say goodbye to the reward, but there's always the postal orders and the person who sent 'em.

"And there's always a person with a helping hand, Bill." Peggy crossed to a mirror and examined her face. "A friend in need is a friend indeed, and we've got a friend." She opened her bag and applied powder and lipstick and a touch of eyeshadow. "A friend at court one might say. Another clerical gentleman." She considered herself presentable and smirked. "Dear, loyal Bishop Gerry."

"Of course I knew Oliver Hendricks, Peggy dear." Gerald Hurst-Hutchings still called himself bishop, though he'd been defrocked and discredited and booted out of the Church of England months ago.

However, though Gerry was out, you can't keep a really bad man down and his lordship appeared to be thriving. He owned a house in Hampstead, he wined and dined with the nobility and gentry, he kept his fingers on the pulse of things. He also had a soft spot for Peggy and welcomed us effusively.

"Poor Oliver and I were curates together at Saint Cuthbert's, Devonshire Place." Gerry was almost as fat as Peggy and like many stout men he could move like a cat. His feet seemed to glide across the carpet as though castors were fitted to their shoes. "Yes, those were happy days at Saint Cuthbert's.

"Two eager young servants of Christ united in His love and stewardship." Gerry had got the sack for dipping into a restoration fund. The Press had labelled him 'The Unjust Steward,' but I didn't mention the fact. I wanted to dip into his lordship's own funds. His store of information.

"Oliver Hendricks was a little too eager perhaps. He came from the Outer Hebrides and was related to the Stuart-Vail family, who you may have heard of, Bill."

"The Lords of Rhona." I broke in because I'd read a history of Rhona once. A squalid account of betrayals and persecution and religious intolerance. "Isn't a woman the head of the family now? Lady Elizabeth?"

"Do stop interrupting his lordship, Bill." Peggy hadn't realized the importance of Hendricks' birthplace. The postal orders had all originated from the Hebrides or North-west Scotland, and women tend to be less law-abiding than men. Also more inclined to avoid adverse publicity. Lady Elizabeth might have condoned the *Vicar's* indiscretions and sent the orders to keep him under wraps.

"Lady Elizabeth was Oliver's half-sister. Their father had an unfortunate liaison with a crofter's wife and he was born out of wedlock." Gerry shook his head in ponderous disapproval. "So sad. He was given his mother's name, but lived in the castle and was treated as one of the family. Maybe shame set him off on his unfortunate venture. Maybe he was always slightly *fey*; many Scots are."

"Unfortunate venture!" I ignored Peg's snort and interrupted again. "That's a mild way to describe a series of brutal murders, Bishop."

"Murders, Bill! I'm not talking about murder and in my view Oliver Hendricks was not responsible for his crimes." Gerry pressed the switch of an intercom set, and demanded coffee and an assortment of cakes when a voice answered. "I was referring to Oliver's crusade in South America which ended so tragically.

"And now to business, my friends." Though the voice was unctuous as ever there was a threat behind it. "You want to know about M.M., and I'm prepared to tell you what I know. For a consideration of course.

"Would three hundred pounds be convenient?"

It wouldn't and I'd never heard of any M.M. I was about to tell the avaricious swine to go to hell, but Peggy trusted him. She was already writing a cheque when a person of indeterminate sex appeared wheeling a trolley.

"Thank you, Leslie, and those éclairs look quite scrumptious." Gerry beamed at his attendant who was dressed like a Regency footman and had long blonde hair and smelled strongly of Chanel Number 7. "Oh, don't bother to pour. I'll be mother."

The male or female impersonator, I couldn't tell which, departed and *Mother* reached for Peggy's offering before lifting the coffee pot.

"Three hundred it is, dear." He had checked the amount and tucked the cheque away in his wallet. "I don't know why you're interested in Hendricks, Bill, and I don't want to know. A burnt child fears the fire." His podgy hand looked slightly tremulous as he filled the cups and shovelled four spoonfuls of sugar into his own.

"Yes, a burnt child, Peggy, and Oliver Hendricks was burned badly." He sipped at the syrupy liquid, munched a chocolate éclair and began his sordid story.

Before falling foul of the Church Commissioners, Bishop Gerry had got on in his profession and Oliver Hendricks had consulted him as a spiritual superior. The canon was bored by his parishioners and All Saints Sodbury-on-Thames, and you couldn't blame the poor sod for that. He told Hurst-Hutchins that he wanted to cast Christ's net in deeper waters and Gerry suggested Nuevo Leon as a fruitful fishing ground. Hendricks accepted the bishop's advice and hurried off to spread the word.

The capital of Leon was called La Libertad, but liberty was one of the many things it lacks. The secret police were an efficient body of men, though rather trigger-happy.

Hendricks wrote to his mentor at frequent intervals from the City of Freedom. He didn't actually tell the mentor what he was up to, but Hurst-Hutchins read between the lines.

Canon Hendricks didn't confine himself to preaching the Gospel. The conditions he found in Leon sickened him and he preached revolution. After a few months every local malcontent flocked to his mission station and they brought offerings. Bundles of pesetas . . . The same bundles I had found in Oliver's desk. Money to buy arms to overthrow the forces of oppression. Money placed in the desk which was wisely shipped to Brazil in case the authorities rumbled him.

I think it's probable that Hurst-Hutchins informed the Leonian embassy about his friend's activity for a decent fee, but there's no point in being uncharitable. It's certainly unwise to make accusations against a useful informer, however dislikeable the informant may be.

In any event, the last letter Gerry received from Libertad suggested that Hendricks had been rumbled. The local Gestapo were on to him and he decided to hook it up the Selva River and enrol recruits for his Peasants' Revolt.

What a hope! Hendricks must have been a fool as well as a fanatic. I know the Selva River and there aren't any peasants capable of revolting. The word Selva simply means *forest* and its inhabitants are primitive forest Indians armed with blowpipes. The recruiting officer soon discovered that his Holy War was a non-event and he reported what had happened in another letter written months later.

Canon Hendricks had travelled five hundred miles upstream

and his original followers had died or deserted him. He was alone and starving and riddled with fever. He was dying himself when a saviour appeared.

"A saviour whom he didn't actually name but referred to by the initials M.M." Having finished his coffee and a second éclair Hurst-Hutchins had opened a drawer and was scanning the correspondence.

"Oliver was naturally grateful at first, but when his fever abated he realized that M.M. was a monster of cruelty, who maltreated his native bearers abominably." The bishop lowered the page and signed. "I won't distress you with details, Peggy, but there were daily floggings and M.M. found it amusing to reward idleness by doses of castor oil. Being a kindly soul, Oliver was naturally horrified and when the party crossed into Brazil he decided that he could stand no more. While M.M. was drunk he made off and he took something with him.

"Something which M.M. had stolen. A religious relic of inestimable value. A golden orb, crammed with gem stones." The bishop lowered the papers and helped himself to a cream bun.

"That's the end of the correspondence, Bill, but not the end of the story.

"Hendricks called on me when he returned to England. He asked for advice and I failed him. My personal affairs were too pressing. That unfortunate misunderstanding about the restoration funds.

"How lacking in charity Christian people can be, Peggy. How cruel and suspicious." He tried to appear martyred, without success. He looked what he was. An unctuous crook who would have flinched the widows and orphans funds if he'd got his fingers on them.

"Yes, I failed my dear friend in his hour of trouble. Oliver told me that he had managed to ship his desk home, but the pesetas were worthless and the Leonese government had been deposed. His crusade had come to nought, but he still had M.M.'s treasure."

Treasure! The very word excited me, and I asked Gerry for details. They were not forthcoming.

"I never saw the object, Bill, but I think I know what became of it. Oliver was terrified of the man he called M.M. He believed that M.M. was that rarity; a truly evil human being, who would hound him to the ends of the earth to recover his orb.

"Poor Oliver was barely coherent and I'm sorry to say that I dismissed him rather abruptly. May God forgive me." His podgy hand made the sign of the cross. "I told Oliver that there was one place where no one would find him; the Isle of Rhona.

"Just an excuse to get rid of him, as I was expecting a visit from my accountant, but a very strange thing happened. Oliver Hendricks went down on his knees and asked me to join him in a prayer to Saint Freda.

"An impossible request. I was troubled by lumbago and Freda is a very minor saint who has never been placed on the Anglican calendar, but Oliver clutched my arm and tried to pull me beside him.

"Don't you believe that a material object can possess supernatural forces?" he asked. "Don't you also believe that such forces may be rendered harmless by holy water . . . the shrine of a saint?"

"I told him that anything was possible, and he was hurting my wrist. He stood up and walked away without another word.

"'That was the last I saw or heard of Oliver Hendricks, Bill, and you've had your money's worth, Peggy. I shall now give you a piece of advice *gratis*.

"I do not know why you are interested in Oliver and I do not want to know, but I beg you to leave well alone." For once Hurst-Hutchins' false unctuous tone vanished and he sounded completely sincere.

"We are three of a kind, my friends. You are criminals and I was an unjust steward. We fear the law of the land, but there is an eternal law which is far more frightening.

"The powers of God. The torments of damnation." The bishop lowered his face and when he raised it I saw that there were tears trickling down his cheeks. "I said that Oliver was not responsible for his crimes, but someone . . . something killed those unfortunate women and I think it may have used Oliver's body as an instrument.

"Forget him, Bill, forget M.M. and his treasure. Don't go near the

Isle of Rhona and confine your activities to petty misdeeds." His normal manner returned for a moment, but only for a moment.

"Hendricks was a priest and so am I. We were trained to recognize the forces of darkness and when I heard about those terrible murders I had a revelation . . . a sort of image showing me what must have happened.

"The Oliver Hendricks I knew was not a murderer, but a victim. He challenged the Prince of Evil and he lost the battle. You can't blame a knife or a gun for causing death. Condemn the hand which used the knife . . . The finger that pressed the trigger. Oliver couldn't help himself; he was possessed by Satan." The interview was almost over, and Gerry glided to the door.

"Please take my advice, Bill. Please don't risk hell fire, Peggy. For some reason I value our friendship." He opened the door and smirked at Peg. "You've got a hearty appetite, my dear, but don't sup with the Devil."

Six

Gerry Hurst-Hutchins couldn't or wouldn't tell us more and I considered what we had learned while driving back to Feltonford. I didn't take his warning seriously, of course. Gerry might claim to have had a knowledge of evil, but he was a crook and all crooks are superstitious. That's why many of them are compulsive gamblers. You can't lose if the cards are running in your favour. You can't escape if your number's on the bullet.

Possession by the Devil, indeed! Oliver Hendricks had lusted after M.M.'s golden treasure and its precious stones. He had become a murderer because he was deranged from the start and his privations in Nueva Leon had knocked him round the bend. The eager young servant of Christ had hoped to start a bloody revolution. A blood-bath across England, Scotland and Wales had been the next best thing.

"Shut up and let me concentrate, Peggy." She had started to say that maybe we'd better leave well alone, but I cut her short. I had to marshal the facts and review the situation.

Oliver Hendricks, the Rector of Sodbury-on-Thames, was a kinsman of the Stuart-Vails who virtually ruled one of the Outer Hebridean Islands. The family and their tenants were largely staunch non-conformists, so why had Hendricks transferred his allegiance to the Church of England?

Hendricks was a mild character according to Hurst-Hutchins. What had made him a revolutionary? Why had the revolutionary become a mass murderer?

According to the Smeatons, Henry Oliver (I still kept thinking of him by his assumed name) had been sent no mail after his death, except a couple of bills for booze and groceries. To the best of their recollection, a poor best, he had never given them any letters with a Scottish address to post.

That meant that Oliver must have kept in touch with his paymasters by telephone and I had a sudden and unpleasant image. An old and immensely stout man gasping into a mouthpiece and informing someone that he was dying. Information which must have pleased the recipient. No more postal orders to buy. No scandal to involve the Stuart-Vail family. Nothing to worry about.

Wrong! I was still so bloody wrong. If Oliver was a multiple murderer no one would have helped him; not even his loving half-sister.

"Unless he wasn't the killer, Bill, but knew who was." Peggy demonstrated her thought reading abilities by interrupting my thoughts. "M.M.? Couldn't that stand for Mass Murder? We know that M.M. was a sadist in South America . . . a monster of cruelty. Isn't it possible that he followed Hendricks to England and carried on in the same way? Hendricks had stolen some relic from him and he was scared. If he was too scared to go to the police he might have made a pact with M.M. and taken the blame. If . . ."

"If you'd stop swilling Guinness you'd be a damn sight slimmer, Peg. If you'd stop spouting gibberish I might have a chance to work out a plan."

What plan? I pulled up outside a roadside pub in the hope that alcohol might set the brain cells creaking.

Henry Oliver, or Oliver Hendricks, had lost a considerable sum by letting his pesetas and postal orders run out of date. Maybe he wasn't interested in worldly goods. Perhaps he was too scared of dogs to walk along to a post office and cash the orders.

M.M. had lost a valuable relic because he'd saved a man's life. I'd lost a hundred thousand quid because I'd slung the man into a council dump.

Such a lot of lolly thrown down the drain, and though Peggy's fears were ridiculous, there was no harm in spending a few quid more.

Only a few. It doesn't cost much to put a short entry in a newspaper, but it might cost lives and I intended to make sure my own life was not jeopardized. I bought a couple of drinks and asked the barmaid for a classified telephone directory.

"We may be dealing with a dangerous man, Peggy," I said. "A man who flogs people unmercifully and doses them with castor oil. Maybe a man with a hatred of your sex who attacks women with knives and hatchets and other instruments. Prudence is required, and I think this should bring our shark to the surface.

"I noted three addresses and composed a message which should appear in *The Times*, the *Telegraph* and something called the *Western Isles Clarion and Adviser.*

"M.M. For Information ref O.H. Urgent you contact . . ." I considered whom should be contacted. It was a million to one that Peggy was mistaken, but I didn't want to meet the Bent Vicar in an unguarded moment.

"CONTACT." I had made my choice and printed the name and address in Block Capitals. "SMEATON C/O NATIONAL-CENTRAL BANK, FELTONFORD, BUCKS."

Seven

The advertisements appeared, but a week passed and no fish rose to the bait. I spent many hours in the public library and gained information on crime, the Hebrides and Nueva Leon. One book was devoted to the Vicar murders and had photographs of the murderer and his handwriting. Illustrations which didn't make sense. Oliver Hendricks was a slim, close-shaven man. He bore no resemblance to the huge, hairy Henry Oliver, but the writing was the same as the writing in the diary. I felt as bewildered as the blind Isaac. "The voice is Jacob's voice, but the hands are the hands of Esau."

I returned the volume to its shelf and returned to the Hebrides.

There wasn't much about the Stuart-Vail clan, but some pretty vague data regarding Saint Freda. A nebulous character who had arrived from Ireland during the fourteenth century floating on an altar stone. Apart from this hazardous voyage, the saint's miraculous powers were demonstrated by the slaughter of animals. Anti-social animals, of course. Foxes, wolves, rats and other vermin all perished on the Island of Rhona and, though the present populace are now largely non-conformist and Freda's name had been struck off the R.C. calendar her shrine was still venerated.

Interesting, but unprofitable, and while I was increasing my knowledge of South America and Western Scotland, Peggy struck up a friendship with Mrs Cynthia Smeaton. I don't know why, as they had nothing in common except commonality, but Peg hoped to learn more about the defunct tenant and I encouraged her. She failed and Cynthia claimed to know no more than what Smeaton had already told me, but I gathered that the two girls had some pleasant chats regarding the shortcomings of their joint partners. I heard a great deal about the habits of Mr Allen K. Smeaton and God knows what he heard about mine.

By the following Wednesday when the library closed at six, all the topics had started to bore me. It was no good reading about Rhona's storm-swept isle. We'd have to go to the place, unless the sinister M.M. put in an appearance. I left the Pub Lib and made for a pub; the Lamb and Flag.

"Who . . . er? What . . . er?" I'd sat down at a table when the phone rang and a barmaid who appeared to be afflicted with a cleft palate answered. "Beast . . . Beaster. Never heard of 'im but I'll ask." She hung the instrument on a hook and screeched across the room.

"Anyone called Beast or Beaster in 'ere?"

The question raised a chorus of chuckles, and I shared the

merriment till I realized the stupid cow was probably deaf as well as virtually speechless.

I stood up and said that my name was Easter and the call was for me. Also that I'd be obliged if she would pronounce my name properly and cut out the *B*. I ignored the asinine cackles, lifted the phone and announced my identity. "William Easter speaking."

"Bill . . . Bill. Thank God you're there, Bill." It took me a moment to recognize Peggy's voice. She seemed to have contracted a cold and her words were interrupted by sniffs and sobs and barely audible. "I'm with Cynthia and Allen Smeaton, darling." In spite of her slurred speech it was the first time in months she'd used the term of endearment and I asked her what she wanted.

"You. Bill . . . We need you, darling, so please come over to the Smeatons at once. At once, Bill . . ." She broke off and I knew that Peggy hadn't caught a cold. She was terrified out of her wits and the sobs increased when I repeated my question.

"Can't talk now, Bill. Not allowed to talk, but hurry." A sob, a pause, a gulp and a whimper. "Something ghastly has turned up."

Something *ghastly*. The English language has become horribly corrupted during recent years. We talk about *what a ghastly party! What a ghastly bore old So-and-So is*. The proper meaning of the word is of course, ghostly and Peg's tone suggested she had used it in that sense.

If so, what ghost had turned up? Though I'm not a churchgoer, I share Gerry's respect for the supernatural and I finished my beer before rushing to Peggy's rescue. I'll take on most human beings, even a homicidal maniac, but my little knife wouldn't be much use against a ghost and after leaving the pub, I drove slowly to Smeaton's residence. My studies at the library had told me a great deal about the folklore of Nuevo Leon and the Island of Rhona, and both areas possess a wealth of sinister legend.

Los Creaturae: the living dead which inhabit the upper reaches of the Selva River. A species of female Zombie, which leave the forest from time to time. First to mate with men . . . then to tear their throats out.

Similar monsters are believed to hover around the coasts of

Rhona. They are known as *Werds* and appear to be a mixture of Mermaid and Werewolf. I hadn't discovered whether they tempted the human race sexually, they were expert throat-tearers.

You may think that I'm fanciful and you may accuse me of cowardice, but I admit that I felt far from happy as I turned into Smeaton's drive. Seven p.m., a fine summer's evening, the pastel-blue paint bright and cheerful. An innocent-looking van which might have been delivering groceries parked outside Oliver's flat. Nothing sinister, but . . .

Groceries? Had Oliver's ghost clambered out of the gravel pit? Was the Savage waiting with his hatchet knife or marlin spike?

The last possibility didn't really worry me. I had a knife of my own and Bloody Mary would deal with any human assailant. But she'd be poor protection against a ghoul, werewolf or the owner of the Evil Eye. According to a book entitled *Legends of the Outer Isles*, the Stuart-Vail family had owned such possessions in bygone days and their eyes did unpleasant things to the persons they rested upon.

All the same, Bloody Mary was all I had and I slipped her out of her sheath. Mrs Margaret Tey couldn't actually be described as a damsel in distress and Mr Easter didn't claim to be a knight errant. But the something ghastly had to be faced and I climbed out the car to face it.

The curtains were drawn, but the house door was unlocked. I opened the door and tiptoed along the corridor. It must have taken me five or six paces to reach the chintzy sitting-room and then I stopped pacing. I stared into the room and I froze because I saw that my supernatural anxieties were justified. Peggy and the Smeatons were cowering against a wall and they had reason to cower. They had companions; horrible companions.

I took a single glance at those grinning jaws, brindled hackles and long, overshot muzzles and then I bolted for safety.

Tried to bolt, and I nearly made it but one companion was too quick. I was on the doorstep when the second werewolf sank its teeth into me.

"Release him, Adam." A voice boomed out, but I was too stunned and in too much pain to see the speaker at first. "Let go of his wrist, boy, but watch him. Watch him well." The horrible brute obeyed, a horrible man emerged from the sitting-room, and I mean horrible. I've seen some ugly customers in my time, but this was by far the ugliest. Though over six feet tall, he was so broad that he appeared squat. He must have weighed far more than Peggy, but all his weight was solid bone and muscle and I'm sure there wasn't an ounce of surplus fat on him. His enormous head was bald and he sported a flowing gingery moustache. A colour sometimes associated with bravery, but more likely denoting rank ill-temper in my opinion. He wore a suit of surprisingly vulgar tweed checks and there was a blackthorn stick in his club-like hand.

"Good boy, Adam. That's my girl, Eve. Stay on guard till I say the word." The man's voice matched his appearance. A rasping domineering voice like an ogre's and I rather imagined that he next words might be, "Fee . . . Fo . . . Fi . . . Fum. I smell the blood of an Englishmun." In a sense they were.

"Adam has had a taste of your blood, Mr Easter, and it's a taste he enjoys. Which his dear wife Eve hopes to share." He grinned at the other beast which had joined him in the corridor and I saw that I'd been wrong. Not were-wolves . . . Not half-human monsters, but monsters and almost as bad. Our tormentors belonged to the genus, *Lupus vulgaris*. Canadian Timber Wolves and perhaps the fiercest animals on earth.

"I see you carry a toy weapon, Mr Easter, and would advise you to discard it immediately. Adam and Eve are obedient creatures, but any hesitation will . . ."

He didn't complete the sentence. He didn't need to. Adam's hackles were still up. The obedient Eve was eyeing my bleeding wrist. I dropped poor Bloody Mary to register defeat.

"Good . . . Very good. I always enjoy seeing a cur cringe, so come and join your fellow cringers."

Cur . . . Cringe. The words infuriated me and if it hadn't been for the wolves, I might have taken a punch at their master; his bulk and his bludgeon notwithstanding. I didn't . . . A warning growl from Adam deterred me and I followed the ogre into the sitting-room and asked him who he was and what the hell he was doing to my wife and my good pals, the Smeatons.

"Margaret Tey is not your wife, Easter." He eyed Peggy balefully; an oriental potentate rejecting an addition to his harem. "The Smeatons are not your good friends, but two miserable dupes unworthy of my consideration." It was Allen and Cynthia's turn to receive a baleful glare; the potentate dismissing two of his less touchable subjects.

"Quite unworthy, so out, both of you. Go upstairs . . . Go to the bedroom and keep out of our way. Eve will see that you stay put." He jerked a thumb towards the staircase and the Smeatons scurried off with the she-wolf at their heels.

"As to my identity." His huge, craggy body seemed to swell and grow taller. "You know who I am, Easter. You wanted to see me and you issued an advertisement in the newspapers, using Smeaton's business address as a place of contact. The bank was closed when I reached this wretched hamlet, but it was not a difficult task to locate the manager.

"Yes, you see me, William Easter." He raised his stick and pushed a curtain aside so that I could get a proper squint at him. A squint which merely increased my revulsion. "You see J.M.M., but he is not here at your service. J. Moldon Mott serves no man."

"Bill doesn't know who you are, sir." Peggy was weeping and she leaned forward as though preparing to wash the fellow's size 13 boots with her tears. "This is Mr Mott, Bill. *The* J. Moldon Mott."

"Exactly, Easter. J. Moldon Mott has arrived to recover his property." He moved closer to the window and like a heavenly portent the sky suddenly darkened and I heard a rumble of thunder. "Moldon Mott." He repeated the title with a deal of pride, but my expression remained blank and his face followed the sky's example and blackened.

"Do you mean to say you don't know who I am? That you've never heard of Mount Mott in Basutoland, or the Mott River beyond Hudson's Bay? That you are unaware of my expeditions to the Pole." There was another clap of thunder and his colour returned to its former gingery hue and he smiled. A pitying smile with little good humour in it, but a deal of contempt.

"Well, I suppose one must make allowances for ignorance and Mrs Tey has told me that you are a petty crook. A felon grovelling for scraps in the gutter who can hardly have eyes for the nobler aspects of life.

"But surely . . . Surely you're not completely ignorant? Surely you must have read the *works*?"

The works. A penny did drop and I recalled my browsings in the library. A line of brightly jacketed volumes issued by an established publishing house and with no doubt as to their author's identity. On each cover Mr Mott proudly surveyed a jungle, desert or mountainous landscape. He wore shorts and sun helmets, climbing boots and anoraks, and a rifle was usually slung across his shoulder. Behind him groups of natives stood in attitudes of awe, adoration and abject terror. The natives' colour varied from brown to black, and yellow to khaki, but the general format of the books was always the same and I even remembered a few of the titles.

MOTT'S WANDERINGS IN CENTRAL AMERICA . . . WITH MOTT ACROSS THE LOST KALAHARI . . . ON THE TRACK OF THE ABOMINABLE SNOWMAN BY J. MOLDON MOTT.

I knew who the Smeatons' visitor was now. Part-adventurer and explorer, part-charlatan and by all accounts a very dangerous character indeed. There were several unpleasant rumours of what had happened to persons who crossed him.

"Mott, sir! You are *the* J. Moldon Mott?" I bowed and held out my hand. "Please accept my apologies, Mr Mott. We only knew your initials and I never suspected who you actually were. Why, I've been an admirer of yours for years and never dreamed that I would have the honour of actually meeting you."

"I bet you didn't, Billy boy." I thought I'd laid it on a bit thick, but his eyes lit up and he took my hand in a crushing grip which was almost as painful as the wolf's fangs. "You made a mistake, but I'm too big a man to harbour a grudge and there's no need for apologies. No time for 'em either.

"Stop that, Adam." The wolf had growled and he delivered a sharp kick in its ribs. "Affectionate beasts, but prone to jealousy. Shot their mother. Reared 'em from pups and they worship the ground I tread on.

"Now, let's sit down and talk business." He motioned me to a chair and lowered himself onto the sofa beside Peggy. "Mrs Tey has already related what happened in the flat and I'm prepared to believe that you didn't find the *Capita*." He cupped his chin on a fist like a grotesque parody on Rodin's *Penseur*. "Hendricks was mentally deranged, but not mad enough to let such a precious thing get mixed up with his other litter." He raised his free hand and thumped the arm of the sofa. "You say that it was not in the desk you rifled, so where is it, Easter?

"Where is my ruddy head?"

Eight

My ruddy head? Mott's statement suggested that he was deranged himself and I gaped at his gingery skull. He then amplified the remark and I believed that he was merely misinformed. "Not my own head, you fool. *La Capita* . . . The head of Eldorado."

A meaningless amplification. Almost everyone knows that *Eldorado* is a Spanish term which can be translated as the *Golden* or the *Gilded* and it does not apply to a single object such as a head. The original El Dorado was a kingdom or a city. A vast, fabulous city roofed with gold and crammed with precious stones.

Fact or fiction? I don't know, though most myths are started by actual events. The story of El Dorado was started by a Spanish soldier who had been abandoned on the Orinoco, and several eminent men believed him and went in search of the city. Most of them came to grief, but the expeditions continued. Philip von Hutten claimed that his followers had caught a glimpse of gold towers soaring above the forest. Sir Walter Raleigh looked for El Dorado and lost his fortune in the attempt. Captain Keymis and Martinez were sure that the city existed and entered it on their maps. It remained on the maps till Friedrich Humboldt checked the location and said that the great, shining town was myth. A delusion created by man's hunger for gold.

I personally believe, or like to believe, that the place did exist once, but the kingdom was destroyed and its treasures stolen long before Raleigh came on the scene.

As for an Eldorado head, however, I'd never heard of any such object and I told Mr Moldon Mott so.

"El Dorado?" He snorted and heaved himself to his feet. "Are you deaf or merely inattentive, Easter? El Dorado is a childish fantasy and I never mentioned it. I was referring to Don Francesco El Dracardo." He obviously expected that the name would make a penny drop, but it didn't for a moment. *Draco* is Spanish for dragon. *Dracardo* might be a Latin-American corruption, but coupled with Don Francesco the name meant nothing to me.

"Ah, I know who Mr Mott's talking about, Bill. Don Francesco . . . Sir Francis Drake." Peggy smirked at her own cleverness. "Didn't the Spaniards call Drake the Dragon?"

"They did, Madam, but what has Sir Francis Drake got to do with it?" The penny had dropped but Peg had pushed it through the wrong slot and Moldon Mott glowered at her. "Drake brought his head safely back to Plymouth Sound. He died with it on his shoulders, but that is neither here nor there." Mott stumped across to a brief-case beside the window. "Drake never visited the Selva River, so please stop displaying your ignorance and have a look at the joker I'm after."

He unzipped his case and held out a photograph for our inspection. The photograph of a death mask. The mask of a man who had been almost as ugly as J. Moldon Mott when he was alive. Though the facial muscles had relaxed when the heart stopped beating, the features suggested abnormal intelligence and cruelty. I felt that their owner would not have been a character to fall foul of.

"That is Don Francesco El Dracardo, Easter. An assumed title and an assumed name. No one knows what he was originally called, but he was definitely a member of the Spanish expedition which left Panama in 1524 to extend their American conquests. An expedition which was routed and the survivors fled back to the isthmus like whipped curs.

"How dare you, Adam?" The wolf shared my resentment to the expression *cur* and Mott silenced its growl with another kick.

"Keep quiet and lie down over there." He pointed at a corner and the beast slunk away.

"El Dracardo was not amongst the survivors, however, though he did survive. He was captured by a tribe of hostile Indians, but by sheer force of personality managed to gain an ascendancy over them. A man rather like myself it appears." He spoke with pride and as I looked at the image in the photograph, I remembered Hendricks' letter to Gerry Hurst-Hutchins and was prepared to agree with him. Mott had treated his bearers to unmerciful floggings and doses of castor oil. El Dracardo would probably have used even harsher methods.

"Extreme intelligence, extreme courage and the capacity to overcome every hardship and difficulty. Yes, very much like myself. Far ahead of his time, though he lacked my cardinal virtue; modesty." The pompous braggart sounded completely sincere and I knew he was mad.

"Once he had gained the Indians' support, Don Francesco didn't wait for the Spaniards to return. If he'd surrendered to a second expedition he might have been charged with desertion and certainly for heresy. His followers had started to believe that he was a god, and he fostered their belief. Under similar circumstances I would probably have acted in the same way."

I bet you would, I thought, though I kept my mouth shut. Peggy interrupted him because she had a question to ask. "Is all this true, Mr Moldon Mott? Has it been written down in the history books?"

"The facts are true, Madam. They were pieced together during months of patient research and incredible dangers. They will shortly appear in the only history book which matters. MOTT'S TRIUMPHS ON THE SELVA RIVER; due to be published in most civilized countries next October." The author of the triumphs smirked and paced the floor.

"From local legends which had been passed down for generations, I established that Dracardo, as his adherents called him, assembled a fleet of canoes and sailed up the Selva. That he crushed every tribe which resisted him and recruited the prisoners into his army. That eventually he halted and founded a kingdom.

"Not El Dorado as you ignorantly believed, Easter, but a

kingdom of gold just the same." Mott continued to pace the floor, his brow wrinkled and his fists clasped behind his back. He obviously imagined he resembled some grave scholar deep in thought. His progress made me think of the frustrated shambling of a caged ape.

"Francesco Dracardo's kingdom covered a large area and he ruled it firmly and paternally. His subjects were simple aborigines, but he taught them to mine gold, and even instructed them in other sciences; engineering, medicine and architecture.

"You are accusing me of exaggeration, Easter. You say that J. Moldon Mott is a romanticist." Though I hadn't said a word for at least five minutes, he glared at me. "You are wrong, however. That photograph proves you are wrong, my friend." He didn't use friend in any friendly sense, but nodded when I picked up the print again. "When my researches were completed, I followed Francesco Dracardo's course up the Selva. Below a mountain called *La Vista del Paraiso*, The Window of Heaven, I discovered the ruins of his city. Amongst those ruins I located his head." He crossed over to me and jabbed a gnarled finger at the print. "The work of a native craftsman, but one of the valuable objects on earth. Though I had no equipment to test the metal, the exterior is almost certainly pure gold. The interior crammed with Brazilian diamonds and emeralds of the finest quality. A thing of imperishable beauty . . . a work of art . . . Also a religious relic of sorts."

Of sorts. I wanted to ask why he had added the qualification but he continued without letting me put a word in. "Francesco Dracardo was executed four centuries ago, his empire died with him, but his spirit is said to live on.

"Why was Don Francesco executed?" Though Mott had ignored my question he considered one from Peggy. "I'm not sure, Mrs Tey, but I suspect he ordered his followers to kill him. That he believed his supernatural powers stemmed from the Devil and he was unworthy to live." Mott moved to Smeaton's sideboard and poured himself a large brandy.

"He called himself Dracardo, the Dragon, remember. Strange how dragons have always been regarded as symbols by races who have never encountered a large lizard." He added soda to his cognac.

"No, I can't tell you how Don Francesco met his end, Mrs Tey, but the corpse was probably decapitated after death and that image was taken from the *capita*." He smiled at the joint use of the term.

"Cheers!" Though we had nothing to toast him with he raised his glass ceremoniously and knocked back half its contents in a single gulp. "I do know, however, that after all those centuries his terror remains. It took me four days to persuade a group of Indians to lead me to the grave and recover the relic. They said that *El Dracardo's ghost* still walks the ruins of *La Vista del Paraiso*. That his head contains a guardian."

Four energetic days, I thought, while he paused to finish his brandy. The thud of Mott's fist and the swish of a whip, but savages have to be kept in line and that golden orb was a worthy line of investigation.

"The chief of the tribe finally led me to the place and I unearthed the relic beneath a carved slab." He continued his lecture, but I wasn't really interested. I did believe he had located one of the most precious objects on earth and I just hoped that it wasn't back in the earth. Squashed flat by a hydraulic ram and tossed into the gravel pit.

Hardly likely. According to Hurst-Hutchins, Oliver Hendricks had stolen the thing and intended to give it a wash and brush up in Saint Freda's holy water on the Isle of Rhona.

If so, no harm would have been done, but why was Mott rambling on about his discovery? It was the re-discovery that mattered and, though Peggy had probably told him our intentions I was prepared to talk business with J. Moldon Mott. He might not be responsible for the Vicar murders, but I was curious to know where he had been when the murders were committed.

"I had just read the inscription on that slab, Mrs Tey. I was prising the stone aside when the chief cried out and a jaguar leaped down on us. A huge ferocious creature, but he didn't daunt me. I dropped the crowbar and grabbed my trusty Gurkha kukri which I always carry on such expeditions. One single flail and . . ."

Mr Mott was overfond of his own voice and I was getting bored by his voice and his exploits. I ignored the wolf crouching against the wall. I stood up and joined its master at the sideboard. I stared at the master and said he'd been a damned fool. Old Dracardo's relic must have been one of the most important archaeological finds ever, on a par with the Rosetta Stone. His feat would have earned him a place in history. His name might have lived forever, so why . . .

"Why the hell did you let Canon Oliver Hendricks lay his squalid hands on it?"

"Because I was a fool, Easter." I'd expected a display of anger but only received an abject groan reminiscent of Allen Smeaton. "I have many virtues, but a single weakness. I suffer from a child-like belief that White Men should stand together." The charitable believer, who thought it amusing to dose lesser breeds with aperients and strap 'em to a flogging post, groaned even more abjectly. "Yes, a sad weakness, my friends. Faith in my fellows . . . A desire to help those in distress." The brute sounded so sincere that I almost forgot he'd terrified us with a brace of timber wolves.

I fixed myself a stiff whisky and waited to hear what helpfulness had got him.

The Selva is an odd river and it divides on its way to the sea. The main branch continues due east to La Libertad, but a secondary stream turns south and joins the Amazon.

Moldon Mott decided that Brazil would be a safer exit than Leon. He was proceeding down the southern route with a song in his heart and the treasure in his canoe when he encountered a wreck. The wreck of a man crawling along the bank on his knees. Mott's binoculars revealed that the man was white, and being a good Samaritan (his description, not mine), he ordered his paddlers to rush to the rescue; an order which cost him dear.

The man was, of course, Oliver Hendricks, and when he became strong enough to listen, he listened to the account of Mott's triumphs. When he became strong enough to reason, he attempted to reason with his benefactor.

The canon did not approve of the way Mott treated his natives. It was wrong to beat them. Cruel to force feed 'em castor oil, though he understood the reason for such cruelty.

"I had told him what I knew about El Dracardo and the inscription on the stone, which was a warning not to remove the relic, and the fool considered that the Indians might have been correct. The orb did contain a guardian; a tempter which had corrupted me by greed and arrogance." Mott's normal arrogance returned and he poured himself another tumbler of brandy. "Hendricks said that I was a grave robber, and I should have heeded the warning. That I had stolen an object which was basically evil, but might be turned to good. He then made a proposition which I found funny at the time . . ."

The proposition was that the evil object should be put to good work: Take the thing to Rio, have it valued and sell the gold and the jewels to the highest bidder. That cache of diamonds and emeralds could buy enough arms to start a revolution. El Dracardo's head would send the oppressors of Nueva Leon packing. The true Window of Heaven would open and a Kingdom of Brotherly Love be revealed.

Moldon Mott laughed. He wasn't going to squander fame and fortune by freeing any oppressed Leonians. He told Hendricks to have his own head valued, and he was still amused when they reached civilization. A shanty town with one hotel and a railway halt.

Amusement which ended when he woke up two days later and discovered what had happened. Canon Hendricks had purchased drugs to ensure his benefactor slept soundly and popped them into the benefactor's sundowners. While the benefactor slumbered the canon had removed Mott's money belt and paid off his bearers. He took Mott's head to the station and boarded the next train. He left Mott just enough funds to settle the hotel bill and buy a railway ticket, but that act of mercy didn't really help J. Moldon Mott. The rains had started and there wouldn't be another train for months.

It took Mott some time to arrive at the port of Belem, and the local consul had to ship him home as a Distressed British Subject on a tramp. Before the tramp sailed he learned that Canon Hendricks had departed long ago on a speedy cargo-liner. The thief and the treasure had vanished to God knows where.

"Where, Easter . . . What could he have done with it, Mrs Tey?"

He looked like a gingery Othello unable to comprehend Iago's perfidy. "From what you told me before Easter arrived it seems clear that Oliver Hendricks must have been a homicidal maniac, though I never suspected he was violent. I never suspected he was a thief, if it came to that. The murders don't interest me unless they can give us a lead to his other activities, so what happened? Where was he from the time he landed in England to the date he took up residence here?"

"Bill thinks he was in Scotland, Mr Mott. On an island called Rhona." Peg opened her mouth as usual. I would have kept quiet till we'd made a pact with Mott. A firm agreement that if the head was located, it would be sold and the proceeds divided three ways.

But Peggy was still hypnotized by the man and she started to blurt out everything we'd discovered. The conditions in the flat, the diary, the letter to Hurst-Hutchins, the state of the body and what Smeaton had told me.

"Hairiness . . . abnormal hairiness." Mott suddenly raised his hand and pointed at the recumbent wolf. "Also a terror of dogs. Could Hendricks have opened the head without taking precautions, do you think? Had he the courage to challenge Dracardo's guardian?"

"But didn't you open it yourself, Mr Mott. Didn't you have a look at them gems?" The customary gleam of lust came into Peg's eyes, as she mentioned the stones.

"No, Mrs Tey. I may be a brave man but I am not foolhardy. I intended to open the relic before Hendricks drugged me, though only when . . .

"The desk is still down there, you say, and I think we should try a little experiment." He put two fingers in his lips and gave an ear-splitting whistle. A summons for the she-wolf to join us and she obediently appeared and rubbed herself against his thigh.

"Yes, an experiment in extrasensory perception. The flat has been spring-cleaned, but animals are far more instinctive than men; wild animals especially. They have inborn warning devices which mankind lost, so let's see what those devices tell them." He retrieved his blackthorn cudgel from the sofa and walked to the basement door. "Probably nothing, as this couple are domestic pets. I said that I shot the mother before they were weaned and had to hand-rear 'em.

"Come on, Evie Sweet." He opened the door and coaxed the pets forward. "Down you go, Adam and report back to Daddy. Down, I say and quick about it." The animals hesitated and he raised his voice and his stick.

"Go down or I'll sell you to a circus.

"That's better." The threat had been understood. Both wolves had vanished through the doorway and Mott lowered his cudgel.

"Now, to terms." He smiled at us. "You should have a pleasant stay on Rhona, and the weather is usually good in August. You'll find that I'm a generous master. Return the head to me intact and you will receive one tenth of what I get for it.

"A princely offer, Billy Boy, and if you refuse, this is the time to say No. I feel certain Rhona is the location and I can easily hire another brace of petty crooks to do the job for me."

Princely! The mean offer of a mean, bullying man. I was about to say so, but there was no opportunity. Pandemonium stopped me. The wolves had discovered something interesting in the basement, or perhaps something had discovered them. I heard an eager yelp from Adam. I heard Eve deliver a sharp keening bark. We all heard the sounds of excitement and within seconds the beasts appeared and they were crazy; completely mad. Adam came first, but his mate was close behind and she grabbed his neck in lustful frenzy. He screeched and fled to Daddy for protection.

Daddy flailed out with his bludgeon, but the blows didn't calm Madam Eve. She neglected her stricken husband and turned on Moldon Mott, though we didn't stop to witness the end of the fracas.

J. Moldon Mott could look after himself and I wasn't getting involved with his timber wolves; nor was Peggy. We were both out of the house and into the car before the disturbance ceased.

Nine

I was certain that there had been no living creature in the basement to cause the wolves' behaviour, but I share Mott's view that some animals have a sixth sense which most human beings have lost, and not only animals. I possess something of the kind myself. I had a strong hunch that our next port of call should be the Island of Rhona, and we didn't delay. We packed a couple of suitcases, left my car at Cleveland Avenue and rang for a mini-cab.

There was light rain at Euston, but it increased during the night. Rain which fell in torrents when we boarded the ferry from Oban and didn't slacken during the voyage. I had heard that the Hebrides are very beautiful, but I didn't see them. I hardly saw a thing till we clambered ashore at Drabster; the only town on Rhona, and as drab as its name. When I asked a dock official about accommodation, he said that Mrs Mackenzie might oblige. We stumbled through the deluge to the shelter of her wing.

The Hotel Mackenzie had a room, but precious little else to offer. When I asked for a drink the proprietor smiled and gave me a knowing wink. "Aye, I ken yer, Sorr. You're like me hubby; a devil for yer tea." Her smiled vanished after I said that I wasn't like her husband and I didn't want tea. It was eleven o'clock; opening time, and I was soaked to the skin. I wanted a large whisky, so where was the bar?

There was *nae* bar and Mrs Mackenzie disapproved of alcohol. She wouldn't even direct me to the nearest pub, but was eager to stuff Peggy with home-made scones. I left them and braved the elements again.

There was a pub some distance down the road, but I saw another place of business, and went in and bought a ten-pound postal order and a registered envelope. A transaction which raised no comment, but when I'd filled in the address and handed it over to the counter clerk, she asked whether I was staying at the castle. Was I a friend of the family?

I gave a mumbled reply which meant nothing, but I knew what the questions meant. The girl had seen other envelopes addressed to Henry Oliver and I'd hit pay dirt. She might have told me who the senders were, but I don't believe in rushing my fences. I pocketed a receipt and made for the Thistle Inn.

The door I opened was labelled "Snug", but the room was as cheerless as a Welsh chapel. A turf fire clock ticked loudly, but the crone behind the bar took my order in silence. Her only other client was a sad-looking character with one hand clutching a wine glass and the other pressed against his forehead.

Not the old Lamb and Flag, but frequenters of public houses are rarely lonely and the climate is a sound gambit to open a conversation. If you start with a political or a religious opinion you're liable to meet hostility, but no one can be offended by a comment on the elements; so I thought.

"What . . . What, did you say?" I'd merely remarked that the rain seemed rather abnormal for the time of year, but the effect on my fellow toper was extraordinary. The stem of the wine glass snapped between his fingers. He lowered his other hand and stared at me in the same way Allen Smeaton had done while admitting his trouble. "Raining. Always rains up here . . . Foul weather . . . Foul place . . . Foul inhabitants."

Strong language, but I thought about Mrs Mackenzie's hospitality. I took a squint at the taciturn crone and said that I'd only been on Rhona an hour, but was prepared to agree with him.

"One hour, sir. A short sentence, but you'll learn before long. I've been trapped here for two months and there's no escape for me." He groaned and then muttered to himself, repeating the word *foul*. "Foul prison . . . foul people . . . foul injustice."

I appeared to have met the local loonie, but I apologized for making him break the glass and offered him a refill. "You wish to buy me a drink? You are prepared to sit down and talk to me." His eyes lit up like a spaniel's being promised a walk. "Thank you, sir. A small Sauterne would be most acceptable. The pleasure of your company might save my reason.

"Thank you again, sir." I had supplied his requirements and his winsome smile increased as I sat down at the table beside him. "I imagine you are a tourist as all the reporters left after the hearing. I am sure you cannot know who I am, or you would not be sitting with me, so allow me to show you." His hand trembled as he reached in a pocket and held out a visiting-card.

"Glad to meet you, Doctor." The card stated that he was Dr Anthony Cayne, M.D., F.R.C.P. and had a number of other qualifications I didn't recognize. "My name is Easter . . . William Easter, and my wife and I are on holiday."

"Then I'm afraid you have started your holiday badly, Mr Easter. Wise men do not drink with lepers." He took a sip of wine and I drew back hurriedly. Leprosy can be highly contagious, though I couldn't see any signs of disease on him.

"Oh, do not worry about your physical health, Mr Easter, I spoke figuratively. Poor Tony Cayne is a social leper. He bears the brand of his namesake upon his forehead. "Women make the sign of the cross when they see me in the street. Children run from me and men spit at my shadow. I am accursed, Mr Easter, I bring bad luck. I possess the evil eye."

"Come off it, Doctor." I looked at his eyes, which appeared harmless enough though the irises were pale blue; a colour several prominent murderers are said to have shared. "A joke's a joke, but what's really upsetting you?"

"Persecution, sir. A witch hunt started by Hector Grant and continued by gangs of mindless barbarians." He delved in another pocket and produced a crumpled copy of the *Outer Isles Clarion*. "I suppose the story has not appeared in the national Press, but this should show you how terrible my sin has been." He spread the paper on the table and one glance showed that I hadn't introduced myself to the village idiot. As in the post office I'd hit pay-dirt.

Two photographs were displayed on the front page of the *Clarion*. One of them of Dr Cayne and the other of a grim-looking type with a lantern jaw. Headlines above the picture stated, BAILIFF'S EVIDENCE REFUTES CLAIM. CRIMINAL CHARGES CONSIDERED. A line of print below the photographs advised the reader to turn to Page 4.

I turned and my hopes soared. Canon Oliver Hendricks came from the Outer Hebrides and claimed kinship with the Stuart-Vail family who were the hereditary lords of Rhona, though the present occupant was female as you know; Lady Elizabeth, referred to as the *Dame of the Isles*. The postal orders had also originated from the same locality and the connection seemed obvious. Lady Elizabeth and her clan had sent money to help their erring relation, though they knew he was the Vicar. Don't ask me why, but blood is said to be thicker than water, as one says, and clan loyalty is a force to be reckoned with. The story on Page 4 proved just how strong.

Dr Anthony Cayne was either a fraud or a much maligned man. Some years ago, at about the same time Oliver Hendricks flinched the Dracardo head from Moldon Mott, the doctor found evidence suggesting that he and not Lady Elizabeth was the rightful owner of the island. He searched long-forgotten records, he discovered more evidence. He consulted solicitors and allowed them to issue a writ on his behalf.

The poor booby should have known better, of course. One lawyer with a brief can steal more than twenty robbers with guns, and Cayne's case was pretty flimsy.

The brief was based on the fact that one Sir Archibald Stuart-Vail had decamped from the island in 1878, taking in tow a chambermaid whose maiden name was Elsie. The happy couple later gave birth to a daughter who married a man called Cayne; the doctor's grandfather.

A rather untenable claim to the succession in my view, and it was shot down during the second day of the proceedings and not by legal precedents. A feudal retainer took the witness stand and he was prepared to trade his own family reputation for the sake of Stuart-Vail's.

The bailiff, Allan Grant, the lantern-jawed character on the front page, swore that Sir Archibald and his run-away bride didn't run far or stay happy for long. On the orders of the current laird, the run-aways had been apprehended and murdered. According to Grant's testimony they had been buried somewhere on the island by his own grandfather, but he wouldn't say where. Such knowledge might embarrass *Her Leddyship*, and the lady had enough worries already. From the day Dr Cayne came to Rhona and spied out the land, Lady Elizabeth and her brothers had gone into retreat and never appeared in public.

If I'd been the magistrate, I'd have demanded that Grant revealed where the corpses were buried and also insisted that Lady Elizabeth, her kith and her kin, did testify, but there wasn't any magistrate. The hearing was conducted by someone called the Fiscal, who shared Grant's loyal feelings and shot Dr Cayne down in flames.

The case was disproven. Tony Cayne had attempted a cruel hoax against an innocent woman. He must remain on the island till it was decided whether criminal charges were to be preferred against him.

"The cruelty, the injustice of it, Mr Easter." The doctor lit a Capstan Full Strength and inhaled deeply. "Allan Grant's vendetta didn't stop after the hearing, you see. Though I mortgaged my practice to pay the legal costs, I face more than imprisonment and ruin. Until it is decided whether I shall be indicted for fraud, I am not allowed to leave this island. I am the Wandering Jew denied the freedom to wander. I am regarded as a bringer of ill-luck; friendless and loathsome.

"No, I have one ally." He glanced at the aged lady behind the bar. "Mrs Alison lets me stay on at the Thistle, though she charges double the normal amount. In a week's time I shall be destitute and then, God help me."

"God helps those who help themselves, Doctor." I had finished the newspaper report and pushed it to one side. "But why are the local people against you? Are the Stuart-Vails so greatly loved in these parts? Did you offend the family during the hearing?"

"They weren't present at the Fiscal's hearing, Mr Easter, and I've never met a single member of the family." He gave a rasping cough either from the strength of the cigarette or emotion. "I called at the castle when I decided to visit Rhona, of course. I hoped we could reach a private agreement, but no luck. I only saw the factor." The term factor was unfamiliar to me, but I knew he was referring to the lantern-jawed individual who'd quashed his case before the Fiscal. "Allan Grant and his wife seemed to be the only servants at the castle, but he didn't behave like a servant.

Grant said that the family were unable to talk to anyone. Apparently there'd been some scandal which distressed them. A cousin or a half-brother was suspected of committing some terrible crimes. Can't remember what the crimes were or what the man's name was, but Lady Elizabeth and her brothers had suffered nervous break-downs and were confined to their quarters."

"The crime was murder, Doctor, and the man's name was Oliver Hendricks." I tried not to show my elation, but it was difficult, because the jig-saw puzzle was fitting together. Allan Grant and his wife knew that Hendricks was the Vicar. That if he was arrested, the shame and disgrace would probably drive *Her Leddyship* right round the bend. The Grants had sent the postal orders to Oliver to preserve the family's honour and remaining sanity, but had they preserved something else? When Canon Oliver Hendricks came to Rhona after robbing Moldon Mott, had he placed the head in their safe keeping?

"Hendricks . . . Yes, you may be right, Mr Easter." Tony Cayne folded the newspaper and stuffed it back into his pocket. "My memory is fading, because everything else Grant told me has come true. He said that if I ever returned to Rhona, the island would be accursed. Saint Freda's holy water would lose its magical powers and allow the beasts to run riot. Grant spoke in all sincerity and he was right. When I did return to state my claim officially, the troubles began. Dogs and other animals go berserk and children and sheep are savaged. All Grant promised came true, but do I look like a monster, Mr Easter? A creature from the pit . . . a vampire?"

"You look like a chap who could do with less cheap Sauterne and have a proper drink, Doctor." I crossed to the bar and asked Madame Alison for a couple of whiskys; a double for myself and a treble for my buddy.

Saint Freda's holy water. I thought about the discredited saint, while she served me. Freda was supposed to have banished animals which were hostile to man from the island, but now domesticated beasts appeared to have become savage.

Savage . . . *The Savage Bent Vicar.* Oliver Hendricks, a left wing cleric who had stolen Moldon Mott's relic to start a revolution. Who had brought it back to Europe and started a blood bath.

Canon Hendricks had lain low in Smeaton's basement and died there. I knew he was dead, no one knew better. There was no living creature in the flat, so what had excited Mott's wolves? Was there a connection between a basement in Buckinghamshire and a shrine on Rhona?

I suppose we should have gone down and examined the flat, but the wolves' behaviour had given us the opportunity to make a getaway from the objectionable Moldon Mott, though I was damned certain he'd follow us before long. I was also certain that little Dr Cayne wasn't responsible for the island's current misfortunes, and I told him so when I brought over the drinks.

"You are very kind, Mr Easter." He expressed his gratitude for both the whisky and my assurance, but I didn't want thanks. I needed knowledge before Mott put in an appearance, and Cayne listened intently to my questions.

"Saint Freda's shrine is in a cave above the castle grounds, and there's a path leading up to it." He was a fund of the sort of information I could have got from a tourist office, but every little helps and I took out my notebook.

The castle grounds were open to the general public every Tuesday, Friday and Saturday during the summer season, but no one had been admitted to the house since the family's sudden illness. The well itself had also been closed by an order of Allan Grant, though Cayne didn't know why.

Neither did I, but I was beginning to have suspicions, and asked him if there was another way to get to the cave.

"I've no idea, Mr Easter. I have never been near the place whatever people say. Lies . . . all lies. Hellish, untruthful rumours that I polluted the stream and drove out Freda's protecting angel." The little man might not have polluted the waters, but he was weeping openly and tears were diluting his Scotch. "But you know that they're lies, Mr Easter, and I'm not alone any more. You trust me. You'll help me to clear my good name and prove my innocence."

"I trust nobody, Doctor Cayne. I suspect everybody. I hope to reveal the truth and expose." A parody cribbed from some French wiseacre, whose name escapes me, though the remark seemed appropriate under the circumstances. I was about to explain my circumstances, but was interrupted by the arrival of two British not-so-wiseacres. Two trolls.

Trolls stem from Scandinavian mythology and they are mountain giants of repulsive appearance and evil tempers. They tramp the hills by night and the ground shakes beneath their footfalls. They bellow curses through the darkness and windows are shattered. They are boorish, uncouth and there is nothing good to be said about them.

Creatures of mythology, perhaps, but the figures who emerged through the doorway did not appear to be human. They both wore deer-stalker caps, sodden kilts and muddy gum boots. They both had faces which might have been modelled out of plasticine by a child. They were both clearly enraged. They both bellowed for alcohol.

"Whusky, Missus." The leading troll lowered a sack onto the floor and leaned heavily against the bar. Number Two removed a shot gun from his shoulder and banged the butt on the bar. "Whusky, Mistress Alison, and quick aboot it."

"Aye . . . Aye . . . Och-aye." The taciturn broke silence and started to deliver what was probably some courteous Highland greeting such as "Welcome hame, me twa bra laddies . . . Hoose lief on th' mountain?"

The only word I really understood was *mountain*, but the trolls were better versed in her lingo and their brick-red faces became even redder.

"Death walks the mountain, Missus Allison." The leader thumped the counter with a fist as big and gnarled as J. Moldon Mott's. "Me and Fergus have been up on the braes of Ben Gracken and f'what did we find there?" I won't try and reproduce any more of his repellent dialect and his emotions couldn't be reproduced. Rage possessed him.

"The fiend's at work again and we've a score to settle." He stopped and pulled a dripping red and white object out of the sack. "Two ewes and a lamb with their throats torn to shreds, so where is he, Missus? Where's the Dogger?

"Aye . . . Aye." He had seen Dr Cayne and myself and a sound which was part grunt and part roar burst from his lips. "You've tasted flesh, Dogger, and now you can eat it." He swung round and hurled his burden across the room. The carcase of a lamb which bounced on the table, spattering me with blood and sent Tony Cayne reeling to the floor.

An unseemly display of ill-temper, but worse was to follow. The second troll wasn't satisfied by lobbing dead sheep about. He'd released the safety catch of his twelve bore and the barrels were pointing at the prostrate doctor. "You'll take no more of our flock, Devil. Hence back to hell where you belong."

Troll Number 2 obviously meant business. His spatulate finger was just about to pull the trigger when I stood up, jostled his partner aside and booted him in the balls.

Ten

The second troll did pull the trigger as my foot went home, but he fired high and no one was hurt. The shot blasted a window however, and the rozzers arrived in due course. Three of 'em; two constables and a Sergeant Gilespie. All huffing and puffing and itching to blow the house down.

Gilespie started by accusing the crone of keeping a disorderly establishment, but the old lady became far from silent. She stated that the *Thistle* was a most respectable place of entertainment. She and her late husband had held the licence for over thirty years and never a breath of scandal. The gentlemen had had a friendly discussion and the gun had gone off by accident. Gilespie should leave honest folk alone and start looking for the killer dogs.

As the second troll was still in some pain and unable to speak Gilespie turned his attentions to me, but there was no case to answer. I had merely been startled by the shot and stumbled against the firer.

No, I wouldn't prefer charges against the troll. Our mountain giants, whose names turned out to be Daniel and Fergus Bryde, were incensed by the loss of their sheep and I bore 'em no ill will. Besides a friend in need is a friend indeed, and I might need a few friends on the Isle of Rhona.

Gilespie informed the crone that she'd best watch her step if she wanted the licence renewed. She advised him to perform an impossible act on himself. A battle was won and the boys in blue departed.

"I'm in your debt, sir." Fergus Bryde had recovered the power of speech and he held out his hand to shake mine. "Though you hurt me bad, I'd have killed yon wee blighter if you hadn't got me goolies." He released his grip and glanced at little Dr Cayne who was staring at the defunct lamb and looked even more crushed and abject.

"The pleasure was all mine, Fergus," I said, which was an unfortunate remark, though he took it in good part. "No hard feelings, but I think it's time we had a dram and a chat. I need to know exactly what's going on this island, and you can help me." I offered to buy a round of drinks but the crone insisted they were on the house. "Cheers." We had toasted each other's health, and I tried to talk business. "The Island of Rhona is my concern, gentlemen, though I cannot divulge by whose authority. I will however state that it is a very high authority indeed." An imposing statement which went down well. I could almost hear the trolls' brains creak as they considered what authority. The United Nations—The Director of M.I.5.—The Ministry of Agriculture and Fisheries?

"I am instructed to investigate what is happening on this island and you, gentlemen, are duty-bound to assist me." I gave the Brydes a long, cold stare.

"You appear to believe that Doctor Cayne possesses the Evil Eye, and we shall now establish if that is true. Look him in the eyes and challenge his powers.

"Do what you are told, men." They had lowered their heads and I pointed at a telephone at the end of the bar. "Any delay and I shall inform Sergeant Gilespie that I do intend to prefer charges. Charges of attempted murder with a firearm. A serious offence which will land you behind bars for a long time."

A simple choice between the law and superstition and the law won. The Brydes looked at Cayne and he looked back at 'em. For an instant their trollish features paled at the thought that they might suddenly vanish in a cloud of smoke but only the peat fire smoked and they relaxed.

"Good." I nodded approvingly. "We have now established that Doctor Cayne cannot possess any evil powers or be responsible for the loss of your sheep, so who is? Who or what attacked them?"

"We call it the Dogger, sir. A fiend which drives the collies mad." Though I'd questioned Fergus his goolies were still hurting him and Brother Dan told the tale. Told it badly, but the gist was clear enough. At about the same time Tony Cayne landed on Rhona the dogs became demented.

Sentimentalists claim that a working collie loves his flock and the only reply is *balderdash*. The dog herds sheep on his master's orders, but is a mass of frustrations. Chasing weaker animals may be fun, but biting 'em would be far more enjoyable. If a dog does bite he gets a taste for blood. The shepherd gets an incurable killer which must be destroyed.

That had happened on the Isle of Rhona and it had happened far too long and far too frequently. Already seven children had been savaged and countless sheep torn to death. Half a dozen culprits had been caught in the act and shot. At least another six were suspected, but according to the Brydes there were many . . . many more. In Dan's view the entire canine population had become possessed by the devil, so who had possessed 'em? Who had polluted Freda's well and removed the saint's protection?

Little Tony Cayne, of course. Allan Grant, the lantern-jawed factor or bailiff had originated the theory. An interloper with the name of the first murderer . . . An impostor who had come to flinch the crown of the Honourable Elizabeth Stuart-Vail, Dame of the Outer Isles . . . Mistress and hereditary monarch of Rhona.

"The family became ill, sir." Daniel used the term family as though it should have been prefixed by *Holy* or at least *Royal*. "No one except Allan Grant and his wife knows what their ailment is because no one else has seen them. But I do know that their illness started around the time he got here." He jerked a finger at Cayne.

"I'm not saying that the family are loved or even well-liked, Mr Easter, but we've a duty towards them. They're our lairds and we must show allegiance.

"Master Oliver . . . Oliver Hendricks, her ladyship's half brother. What's Oliver to do with it?" He paused and considered my question. "Oliver Hendricks was the son of the old laird and a local lass. She died and the family always treated Oliver as one of their own, till he did a bad thing." Daniel lowered his voice and I expected to hear about the Savage murders. I was disappointed.

"Master Oliver betrayed her Ladyship. He became a minister of the Church of England." He shook his head in deep disapproval while I questioned him again. "Aye, Oliver did return here once, though only for a week or two. The papers suggested that he might have got up to some doings on the mainland, but I can't believe them.

"Oliver Hendricks adopted a false faith, but he was a kindly soul. He wouldn't hurt a fly let alone murder a woman. At any rate, Oliver's supposed to be dead and we can't blame him for the curse on the island. Oliver didn't poison the water and rob us of Saint Freda's blessing, and it now seems we can't blame him." He jerked a second finger towards Tony Cayne. "So, who is to blame, Mr Easter? Who offended Saint Freda and drove them collies wild?"

"It's not only the collies, Danny." Fergus Bryde had recovered from his injuries and he interrupted and turned to me. "Other beasts have become possessed, sir. Our neighbour, Saul Macalpine, was gored by one of his own heifers. A gentle wee creature, but for no reason . . . no reason we can understand that is, she went crazy and dug a horn into him.

"Saul had to beat her off with a pitchfork, but he still couldn't be controlled. Worth two hundred pounds and he had to shoot her."

"What about Collinson's sow, Fergus?" Dan obviously fancied himself as a raconteur and resented his brother's interruption. "Malcolm Collinson farms over Leddersglen way, Mr Easter, and he loved that old sow as though she were his daughter.

"Nay, better than his daughter. Flora Collinson ran off to London with an English tourist. Malcolm never heard from her again and it's the pig I'm telling you about.

"That old sow had no litter. Pigs can turn savage when they've wean to protect, but she was past breedin' and Collinson kept her on as a pet." Daniel Bryde eyed the body of his dead lamb sadly. "A sore waste of bacon but he couldn't bear to have her slaughtered and his extravagance cost him more than fodder. Like Macalpine's heifer that sow went crazy. She turned on Collinson . . . She tore off his left hand."

"Quiet, Danny." Fergus interrupted again, but not to tell another story. "Haud yer tongue and list." He tiptoed across to the window, though that's an inaccurate way to describe the movements of a hulking clodhopper in gum boots. "All off youse come ower here and list."

I did go over to him. I did list and what I listened to made me regret setting foot on the Isle of Rhona. The rain had stopped, but the sky was still dark and the street was silent and deserted. The whole town seemed unnaturally quiet, but the country beyond the town was not.

From every hill, mountainside and valley I heard the howling and baying of a dog.

Eleven

The Thistle was about half a mile from Mrs Mackenzie's hostelry, but the walk seemed endless. The frantic howling and baying in the distance grew louder and at every yard I began to imagine the dogs had it in for me personally. I crossed the street when a miniature poodle came nosing down the pavement and I broke into a trot at the next corner.

A display of panic which nearly cost me my life. Though I hadn't encountered a single pedestrian, I almost made contact with a motor cyclist who came hurtling through the gloom and missed me by inches. He skidded and then cursed after regaining control of his machine and I caught a glimpse of a long jaw protruding over his collar. Allan Grant, the bailiff, in a hell of a hurry. I cursed back and shook my fist at him as he roared off out of the town and towards the mountains which looked even more sinister in the strange afternoon twilight. Their jagged peaks resembled fangs and made me think of an Irish saying which refers to the three most treacherous things on earth. "Tooth of a Dog . . . Horn of a Bull . . . Smile of a Saxon."

Allan Grant wasn't Saxon and he hadn't smiled when I trotted in front of him. Grant was bloody furious with me, but dogs' fangs had killed the sheep and savaged the children. A cow's horn had stabbed one farmer and a pig's jaws deprived another of his hand. Something had driven the animals of Rhona mad, and I somehow suspected that someone was smiling. I hadn't a clue who the smiler might be, but I was damned glad to reach the shelter of Mrs Mackenzie's cheerless portal.

"I trust you've been having a convivial session, Mr Easter." The lady herself eyed me coldly. "There's nae restaurant, but if yer're sober enough to eat, you'll find sardine sandwiches in the bedroom.

"Watch the stairs, though. There's nae porter to carry yer up."

If there'd been any other accommodation available I'd have told the impertinent hag to go to blazes, but *Needs must when the Devil drives.* I returned her chilly stare and went in peace.

"Bill . . . where have you been, Bill?" There'd been two plates of sandwiches in the bedroom, but only one sandwich remained and Peggy had scoffed the rest. "You've been gone for more than two hours and I was so worried." Peg might have been worried, but she didn't look it. She was sitting in front of the dressing-table mirror combing her ginger hair and bursting with sardines and excitement.

"Did you send a registered letter to Smeaton's address?

"I thought so." She scowled at me through the glass when I nodded. "And you put the hotel address on the back of the envelope, of course, and the girl read it.

"Yes, that's how they traced us and why Mr Gordon came here. He wanted to warn us. To tell me not to go near the shrine . . . Such a good, holy man."

"Who the hell is Mr Gordon, Peggy?" My ruse in the post office had obviously borne fruit. The person who sent the original postal orders had come into the open, but I'd imagined the sender was Allan Grant. The name Gordon conveyed nothing to me.

"James Gordon is the local minister, Bill, and I've never met a more pleasant gentleman." She swung round on the stool and her scowl changed to a smile. "He wants to help us, Bill. He came over as soon as he learned about your letter. Everybody in the town will know you sent it by now, they'll all be against us except James. He's the one friend we've got. The only person who can help us."

"And what does the Reverend Mr Gordon want in return, Peggy?" I spoke bitterly and I had reason to. Peg was enamoured by gentlemen of the cloth, though that didn't bother me. She could go to bed with Hurst-Hutchins if she wanted, though it was unlikely he'd fancy her. But during the last two hours I'd had a dead lamb lobbed at me. I'd been threatened by a twelve-bore shot gun and nearly killed by the bailiff's motor bicycle. I'd made friends with the Brydes and Dr Cayne and earned the displeasure of Sergeant Gilespie. I'd achieved quite a lot and what had Peggy done? Mrs Tey had confided in an oily non-conformist minister and spilled the beans.

"I suppose you told him why we're here, Peggy? Told him about the treasure . . . Our treasure . . . Moldon Mott's golden head?"

"I didn't have to, Bill. James Gordon told me." Before I could stop her the greedy bitch stood up and grabbed the last sandwich. "Oliver Hendricks and Mr Gordon had been friends for years and when Hendricks last visited the island he mentioned the relic. He said it was a thing of great beauty, but also a source of evil. He intended to exercise the evil in holy water."

She obviously meant exorcized, but I didn't contradict. I thought of what we had learned and more pieces of the puzzle were fitting together. Canon Hendricks intended to cleanse his ill-gotten gains in Freda's well and with any luck the gains might still be there.

"But the exercise didn't work, Bill, and that's why Mr Gordon confided in me. He had to talk to some third party who can be trusted. He believes that a demon has been released on Rhona, and Allan Grant is screening her." She tried to speak dramatically; a difficult performance when your mouth's crammed with toast and sardines.

"Oliver Hendricks committed those murders because the demon possessed him. Mr Gordon believes that the Stuart-Vails may have been so smitten with remorse that they daren't show their faces in public. He feels sure that someone called Allan Grant sent those postal orders to avoid further scandal. If the murderer were brought to trial, the shame and disgrace could destroy them.

"I told him that Hendricks was dead, of course, but James Gordon said that one death was unimportant. The demon is still at work on the island and he saw her."

"Her?" Though I registered surprise I think it's quite probable that the Devil is a woman, and why not God if it comes to that? Fools who talk about the weaker and gentler sex should check the careers of Boadicea, Elizabeth the First and Catherine the Great. You won't find that much weakness was displayed by that trio.

But though I'm prepared to believe that the Prince of Darkness is a Princess, I could not see a Free Church minister sharing my view and I asked Peg what Satan or Satana looked like.

"I'm trying to tell you if you'll stop pacing about and listen, Bill." I had crossed to the window and saw that the clouds had blown away and the sun was shining. I also noticed that the canine commotion had stopped and there wasn't a bark to be heard.

"You have my full attention, Peggy." I sat down on the edge of the bed and nodded. "I want to know all you learned from Mr Gordon."

Peg had learned a lot. She can be persuasive at times and when he knew we were on to the postal orders and that Hendricks was dead, Gordon had poured out his troubles to her.

Troubles of conscience at first, though they didn't concern me. Hendricks had stolen some religious relic. Hendricks had left the island and was suspected of mass murderer. Grant, the bailiff, had been buying large quantities of postal orders and sending them to an address in England. It seemed clear that the loyal retainer was screening the murderer, so what should the minister do? Go to the police or keep quiet and preserve the family honour.

He didn't go to the police. He went to Freda's well and prayed for guidance.

Low church clerics don't usually set much store on saints or shrines, but James Gordon had lived in the islands all his life and believed that the water did have some miraculous properties.

As I found out later, the shrine is not a well in the usual meaning of the term. The pool isn't fed by an underground spring, but by a stream which trickles down from the moors above. A little, peaty brook which becomes crystal clear when it enters the cave. That probably started the legend of Freda's saintliness, but I personally believe that the stream passes through a belt of sand which acts as a filter.

In any event, the Rev. Gordon reached his destination one winter's evening and flopped down at the edge of the pool. He prayed for God's guidance. He asked Saint Freda what course of action he should take. He dipped his hands into her pure, crystal water.

Pure water! Crystal water! Greasy polluted water! His fingers told him that something was amiss and he switched on a pocket torch to confirm his suspicions. The beam showed that the pool was discoloured and not by peat. Floating on the surface was the mangled body of a rabbit.

That was before the outbreaks of animal violence started and Gordon was more surprised and shocked by the desecration than frightened. A wire grill is positioned outside the cave to prevent unwelcome objects entering the shrine. The defunct bunny couldn't have been washed down, and he could hardly have crawled up the overflow. His head was squashed flat and he hadn't got a brain to guide him.

A mystery, and Gordon remained on his knees considering the solution. He remained on 'em for about five minutes before he realized he was not alone. He didn't see anything . . . He didn't hear anything, but he sensed something. He smelled a smell.

A smell of life as well as death. A pungent, vital smell merged with the tang of rotten flesh. A fox was in the cave and the minister prepared for action. The beast must have been consuming its prey when he disturbed it. He swung his torch around the cave. He grasped a stone to hurl at the desecrator. He raised his arm and the stone dropped from his grasp. He saw what the intruder was.

A masked human figure was seated by the overflow. Gordon felt sure the figure was female and human, though I don't know how. From top to toe the body was covered by a thick plaid hood and cloak and it wore fur gloves. One of the gloved hands was stroking a yellow orb about the size of a football.

Not an attractive female apparently, but Lilith, the Mother of Evil. A beldame with scarlet eyes which glared at him through the slits of her mask and a voice that screeched and gibbered when Gordon stood up and made the sign of the cross.

"Not a natural scream, Bill. James said it was like the cry of a soul in torment and he knew he was in the presence of the Devil." Peggy frowned at my expression of doubt and well she might. Devil indeed! Mr Gordon had surprised some harmless gipsy sheltering in the cave and she'd disturbed the fox before he got there.

"What did Satan-Satana do then, Peg? Blast the minister with her glaring eyes? Haul him off to perdition with her?"

"You are a blasphemous and ignorant man, Bill Easter, and I regret the day I ever married you."

Fair comment! I regretted the day I'd met Peggy, though I hadn't married her. Mrs Tey had a husband already, but I wasn't concerned about him. My interest was orbs. A yellow orb as big as a football and I apologized and asked her what had happened next.

Very little it seemed. Lilith-Satana had closed her glaring eyes when the reverend gentleman made the sign of the cross. Mr Gordon had prudently hooked it and kept quiet till he met up with Peg and discovered she was a sympathetic confidante.

But the time had come for Jimmy Gordon to confide in someone else. The confidant was William Easter. The subject under discussion . . . footballs.

A yellow football . . . The golden head of El Dracardo.

Twelve

Mrs Mackenzie provided another plate of sandwiches, which I made sure Peggy didn't get her hands on, and directed us to Gordon's manse which was a couple of miles to the south. It was two-thirty when we set off and the walk was not enjoyable. The storm had cleared, but a hot sun raised misty patches from the damp earth and the atmosphere was almost as humid as Smeaton's basement had been.

I thought about that basement and what progress had been made since I first stared through the glass door and we'd learned a hell of a lot, though it added up to little.

We'd cleared the flat and disposed of its occupant's body. We knew that the occupant had been Canon Oliver Hendricks, who'd killed at least twelve women and there had been a large reward for the person who located him. A reward which we could never claim since Hendricks had been flattened in the Council's crusher.

We felt pretty certain that the Stuart-Vail family had suffered a breakdown and gone into seclusion when they realized what their relative had done, and that Allan Grant, the loyal retainer, had sent postal orders to avoid his arrest and further scandal. More useless information because we couldn't put the squeeze on Grant or the Stuart-Vails. We'd hidden the evidence.

I'd heard about the outbreaks of animal violence on the island and that little Dr Cayne was believed to be responsible for causing them, though that didn't concern me. My only concern was the golden head, and though Mr Gordon had been in a state of shock after he encountered the mysterious lady in the cave, I was pretty sure he had seen El Dracardo's treasure.

Oliver Hendricks had concealed the golden orb in the cave, and some wandering gypsy had found it. Our only task was to find the gypsy, recover Moldon Mott's possession, and make off before the owner caught up with us.

So simple . . . too simple, though I didn't think so at the time. Lust for gold is an addiction and I was hooked on Dracardo's head. I honestly believed that if Mr Gordon could describe the object in detail I was home and dry. I never imagined that the gypsies might have realized how valuable the thing was or that they could have left the island and sold their loot. I just wanted to hear Gordon's story, and I kept telling Peggy to hurry.

She didn't and I couldn't blame her. The road steepened, the sun got hotter and the midges were troublesome. The local inhabitants call them midges, but I think the definition is incorrect. The creatures which attacked us were like huge flying ants and they stung or bit with hellish accuracy. Mrs Mackenzie had warned Peggy against them and given her a tube of repellent cream and it seemed to keep the brutes at bay. I had no such protection and tried to beat them off with a cap. It proved a poor weapon against the insect world, though I knew its effectiveness against larger foes.

An ordinary cloth cap, but modified on the advice of a Geordie seaman. Geordies are good friends, but dangerous enemies. The cap had three razor blades sewn into its peak.

An uncomfortable walk, but we met a few friendly faces on the way. Dr Cayne furtively posting a letter. Furtively, though he looked more cheerful than when I'd first met him, and I didn't notice any women cross themselves or men spit in his shadow. News travels fast in rural communities. The word had got around that he didn't possess the Evil Eye and wasn't to blame for the island's ills.

I saw the trolls rattling along on a tractor and a flat cart. They both waved and smiled at me warmly.

We also received a smile and a wave from a courteous old buffer mounted on a pony. The wave showed that he'd lost three fingers of his right hand. The smile suggested that he had been a pretty tough cookie in his prime. An arrogant, self-confident smile, but not a Mottish arrogance. Though the rider must have been pushing eighty, I felt he could run rings around Mr J. Moldon Mott.

"That must be the manse, Bill." Peggy pointed at a building ahead though I didn't realize it was a house at first. The place was surrounded by trees and clustered with azalea bushes and looked like a mass of scarlet vegetation.

"It might be better if you wait here and I talk to James alone, Bill. I'll introduce you later, but he has a strong awareness of evil and . . ."

"And might believe I'm another manifestation of Satan." Peggy's an insolent bitch, but she was probably right. Gordon had kept quiet about his experience in the cave, till he found a mother figure to confide in. He might become still more informative to Mother Tey, but hedge at me. "Very well, Peggy. I'll wait till you call, but play our fish carefully. We want to know all about that woman and her yellow football."

Play easy or get into bed with the poor fish, if necessary, I thought as she waddled away down the drive. Peg's infidelities didn't bother me. Gordon could haul her upstairs on his back, though he'd probably break his back in the attempt. I was hooked . . . hooked on gold and diamonds and emeralds. The lovely gleaming head of Francesco El Dracardo.

I lit a cigarette in the hope that smoke might deter the midges, which it didn't. I leaned against a drystone wall and studied my surroundings. Inverlee Castle was visible to the south-west. An imposing pile of Victorian Gothic with mock towers and battlements and the odd flying buttress thrown in for good measure. It looked more like a railway terminus than a seat of the nobility and gentry.

I saw a mounted figure ambling along the road from Drabster. The old party with the crippled hand must have concluded his business in town and be returning to some lovely croft.

I heard a siren bellow and saw the ferry from Oban rounding a headland. I saw a fishing boat bobbing on the swell. I cursed the ruddy midges. I dragged at the cigarette and waited. I shut my eyes and thought about J. Moldon Mott, his treasure of the Selva and the clean pairs of heels we'd show him when the treasure was ours.

I think I dozed off when another hoot of the siren disturbed me. An agonized hoot and I looked out to sea expecting that some navigational hazard was in the offing. Ferry and fishing boat were on collision courses.

I was wrong. Both vessels were safely apart, but the signals of anguish continued. It took me a moment to realize that a siren was not responsible for the clamour. The sound came from behind the wall and my partner was in danger. I discarded the cigarette, pulled off my razor cap and belted to the rescue.

The path or drive to Gordon's manse was over a hundred yards long but I must have broken an Olympic record, and my heart was pounding when I charged through the front door, which had been left open to show a Spartan sitting-room with stripped-pine furniture and religious pictures on the walls, but I didn't stop to examine them. The cries for help came from another door which was also ajar and I hurried on.

Hurried without noticing that the lintel was too low for a normal human being and my head crashed against the beam and I fell sideways against two more obstacles. First a kitchen sink . . . secondly the floor of the kitchen.

A wet, greasy floor . . . A red floor, though I didn't see its colour for a while. The third impact knocked me cold and I never saw that the tiles were spattered with blood.

"Well . . . Well . . . Well." I came round slowly and the first thing I heard was the voice of Sergeant Gilespie. "Caught red-handed, Mr Easter, and I trust you're proud of your handiwork." He pulled me to my feet and I almost passed out again.

A man lay on the floor, and a clerical collar suggested that the man had been the Reverend James Gordon. He was obviously dead though his features appeared to be moving because they were crawling with insects. Above the collar was a gash which only a cliché could describe. His throat had been ripped open from ear to ear.

"Aye, razored, Mr Easter. Repeatedly slashed with that hellish device." Gilespie looked at a constable who was holding my cap. "A brutal murder and there's nothing more to be said."

"We didn't do it, Officer." Peg was leaning against a cupboard. She had stopped screaming but was gulping and sobbing and barely coherent. "He was dead when we got here. You can't blame Bill or me."

"I'm not blaming you, Madam. As a servant of the law I merely investigate facts without emotion and it will be for the Fiscal to prefer charges.

"Providing we manage to get you to court, that is."

Providing! Hope springs eternal and for a moment my hopes rose. Gilespie had imagined we killed Gordon, but it seemed he was becoming doubtful and regaining his senses. I was wrong, however, and his next statements showed how wrong.

"Aye, there's *nae* doot that you're a pair of brutal murderers, but taking you to court may be difficult. The pastor was a popular gentleman. Well-loved by his congregation and they'll take his loss hard. Law-abiding folk up to a point, but there's always a breaking-point, Mr Easter. The camel can carry just so much straw and then . . ." He paused and scowled at the popular pastor's body. "Do I make myself clear?"

He did and I felt sickened and not by the gore. I've seen plenty of gore, but I've also seen a lynching mob in action. The two trolls had proved that the inhabitants of Rhona were prepared to take the law into their own hands and the Forestry Commission had provided 'em with ample timber for gallows.

"We're innocent, Superintendent." Peggy hoped to appeal to Gilespie by raising his rank. "The door was ajar and I came in and waited for Mr Gordon. I must have waited for about fifteen minutes and then I heard those horrible midges buzzing away and went and found him."

"A tissue of lies, Madam." The unemotional guardian of the peace spoke with relish. "I know what happened and I'll make sure that you pay for it."

"Stop hectoring the lady, Sergeant." There was an open door leading to the garden and the character we had seen on the pony appeared. He had a cigar jutting between his lips and his tone was as authoritative as I'd imagined. "And you will pull yourself together and stop snivelling, Madam." He eyed Peggy coldly and she did stop. Her sobs ceased abruptly, and though Gilespie didn't pull his forelock or say *three bags full, sir,* he drew himself to attention and saluted.

"That's better." The old party blew a cloud of smoke across the kitchen. "I shall now explain the situation to you, Sergeant. On my way back from town I heard a commotion and naturally investigated its cause. I found Mr Gordon with this man lying unconscious beside him. I saw this woman in a state of hysteria." He jabbed one of his few remaining fingers at Peggy. "I ascertained that Gordon was beyond medical help and then I telephoned the police station." An impressive old party, though a trifle fond of the personal pronoun. "I have since made further investigations and reached the following conclusions." It was Gilespie's turn to receive a jab of a finger. "This is no ordinary murder and Mr and Mrs Easter, as the woman calls herself, are not responsible for the minister's death."

"Then who is, sir?" Gilespie was still standing to attention. "I thought . . ."

"Don't think, Sergeant. You are incapable of serious thought." My own opinion to a tee and I warmed towards him. "Leave the thinking to those who are trained to think, and only speak when you're spoken to.

"You will stand at ease, have a quick look at the suspects' footwear and then take your assistants outside and examine the evidence."

"At once, sir." Gilespie glanced at our shoes and then hurried off with his constables behind him.

"Not a bad fellow, Mr Easter, but far too full of himself." If gargoyles can smile, our benefactor might be described as smiling. "The insolence of office has gone to the sergeant's head and he needs cutting down to size." My own opinion again and my warmth increased.

"Bhrr . . . It's damned cold in here." Apparently his own warmth did not. Though it was a hot afternoon and he was dressed in thick tweeds he shivered and massaged his hands together. "Poor Gordon took no interest in creature comforts. Hardly ever lit a fire or turned on the central heating, but you'll find things very different in my place.

"Well, Sergeant?" I was about to ask him who he was, but Gilespie returned; a different Gilespie. The sergeant had been cut down to size all right. He looked humbled and defeated and I've rarely seen such a change for the better.

"Yes, I was right of course. I usually am." The old boy nodded complacently without waiting for an answer. "Mr Gordon was killed several hours ago and the footprints show what killed him."

"Several hours ago!" Though the old man was a wise old man I felt sure he was mistaken and pointed at the floor. "The blood is still wet. It hasn't clotted."

"For a simple reason, Mr Easter." A pair of mild, grey eyes twinkled urbanely. "The blood has not congealed because it contained an anti-congealant. I presume you have heard of a substance called Warfarin."

"Isn't it a poison?" Though he was looking at me, Peggy had to display her fund of general knowledge. "Don't they use it for killing rats?"

"Quite right, Madam. Warfarin causes haemophilia when taken in large doses and the rodents die of internal bleeding because their blood becomes too thin. But the preparation is also administered to persons suffering from heart conditions. Warfarin prevents the blood cells furring up the veins and arteries and allows them to flow freely.

"Mr Gordon was troubled by a vascular complaint. He was taking prescriptions of Warfarin. His blood has consequently remained liquid after death."

"Now, I can rely on you to carry out the routine spade work, Sergeant." He turned to Gilespie who was still crushed and abject; a shadow of his former self. "Footprints on the lawn show that the creatures were running towards the screes, so their traces will be lost. Take accurate measurements and photographs of course before you move Gordon's body.

"Do you want your headgear back, Mr Easter?" He nodded at my cap which the constable had lain on the draining-board and grinned when I declined. "No," I thought not. "A strong man armed keepeth his house in order till a stronger cometh." To the best of my knowledge you have no house to keep and razor blades are poor weapons. You need guile to defend you, my boy. We must be as gentle as doves and as cunning as serpents.

"Come along though. There's no point in freezing to death in this ice box. Give me your keys, Gilespie. I'll borrow your car and you can telephone for another or walk back to Drabster. My pony will find her own way home." The wonderful old man strode out of the house, released his steed which was tethered to a tree and climbed into the driving seat of a police Jaguar.

We climbed into the back and he accelerated and drove off at a rate which ill befitted his years and what I imagined to be his official position. Once again we'd hit pay-dirt and made pals with the benevolent Fiscal or the Chief Constable; certainly one of the biggest pots on the island.

So I thought, and I was right in a way. Our benefactor was a big pot, but there was nothing benevolent or pally about him. *Gentle as doves . . . Cunning as serpents!*

Doves may look gentle, but they are extremely fierce birds. Serpents appear cunning, but not a tenth as cunning as our acquaintance.

Old cripped hand could out-fly an eagle and outwit a rattlesnake.

"Sit down and make yourselves comfortable." We had arrived at his residence which was a large modern bungalow, though I wouldn't describe it as comfortable. The central heating was full on, an electric fire hard at work, and the atmosphere was stifling. Also the windows faced south and the sun didn't help matters. I asked whether we could have the windows opened, but the request was ignored and he produced a visiting-card stating his name, former rank and several honours.

Major-General Charles Kirk (Rt'd), C.M.G., D.S.O., M.C., and a foreign title which should have cemented our friendship; Star of Cordelia Robinsonland, 2nd Class.

Cordelia Robinsonland is a damned silly name to call a country, but the star is its highest honour. *Firsts* are only given to heads of state and reigning monarchs.

"A *moderately* distinguished award, Easter, but how did you earn yours?" Though I told him we were members of the same club he wasn't impressed.

"I got my Robinsonland trinket for serving in the League of Nations expeditionary force which pacified the country before the Second World War. You were decorated for a less orthodox service. Political assassination . . . The cold-blooded murder of a president. Correct me if I'm wrong, Billy Easter."

He wasn't wrong though I didn't care for the term cold-blooded. The president referred to was a barbarous tyrant who deserved everything he got. What he did get was a slab of *plastique* which blew him off his palace balcony, but I didn't see how Kirk knew that.

"It is my business to know things, Bill, and I am hardly ever wrong." He moved to a table which supported a fine array of bottles. "I even know your favourite beverages, so let me supply them." Though his back was towards me I was sure he was smiling.

"Malt whisky, Billy me son. Gin and bitter lemon, Peggy dear."

"A refreshing beverage, Peg, which should not harm your already overblown figure, though no ice is available. Putting drinks on the rocks is a barbarous American custom which I deplore."

"Your poison, Bill Easter. Your good health, Peggy Tey." He held out the glasses, delivering mine with his maimed hand which was slightly repulsive. Apart from the missing fingers, the palm was mottled with grey scar tissue and reminded me of a furnace clinker.

"To friendship, Bill and Peggy." He fixed himself a brandy and smiled, though not in a friendly manner. "You will note that I address you by your first names, but I would advise you not to reciprocate and call me Charlie."

"To you I am *Sir . . . Major General* or *General Kirk*."

"Cheers, General." I lifted the glass he'd given me and toasted him. "Here's to the very, very model of a modern major-general, though modern's a bit outdated. You're not on the army list, as your card states. A bit too long in the tooth for active service and the field of Agincourt is over." I grinned and took a swig of Scotch. Though Kirk had got us out of Gilespie's clutches I resented his tone and intended to show it. "Youth is at the helm now, and I want to ask you some questions.

"What are you up to? Who killed Gordon? How the hell do you know so much about us?"

"Let's take the last enquiry first." He might not have cared for the reference to his age, but spoke without rancour. "Your life is an open book to me, Billy. A sordid little book to date, but there are still a few pages which I haven't scanned and that omission must be rectified." He had tossed away his cigar stub in the car and opened a case on the table and helped himself to another. "Yes, only a few pages left and I'm sure they'll be equally squalid." He lit a cigar and leaned against the wall. There was an oil painting behind his back. A portrait of himself in his prime and he looked very impressive. Three rows of ribbons on his tunic, scarlet tabs and highly polished Sam Browne belt and boots.

I felt sorry for the unfortunate drudge who had had to polish those boots, but I wasn't really impressed. The painting seemed out of focus or maybe the heat was affecting my eyes. I felt drowsy and half-asleep and the cigar smoke was forming a cloud. A thick blue cloud which obscured our host's features as he crossed to a desk.

"Yes, only a few pages left," he repeated, "and you can read them aloud to me. My job is to distinguish truth from falsehood and I want to hear the last chapter, Comrade Easter." He bent over the desk and when he straightened up I saw something glint in his horrible, cripped hand. "You can still speak, *Tovarich*, but your muscles are paralysed. The whisky contained a sedative, and this gadget contains a substance which must be familiar to you.

"A substance to make people talk, Billy, so start talking. Your lady lover has already gone to Beddy-Byes, but I'll keep you awake. They say that confession is good for the soul and you've so much to confess.

"That's right. Here's a vein and pop goes the weasel." He had rolled up my sleeve and I couldn't stop him. He dug the needle of a hypodermic syringe into my arm and I did nothing. I heard a clock on his mantelshelf strike the hour . . . I didn't know what hour. I heard Peggy snore and I heard my host's voice. I'm not sure whether I heard him correctly, but if I was right he asked the most foolish question which had ever been put to me.

"Who persuaded you to join the K.G.B., Billy Easter?"

Thirteen

The K.G.B.!!! Major-General Charles Kirk imagined I was a traitor and he'd used a Russian invention to discover he was wrong. Sodium pentothal . . . The truth drug. They say there's no fool like an old fool, and when I was able to think rationally I reminded him of that saying.

Bill Easter a traitor to his Queen and Country! The servant of a bunch of bone-headed Muscovite *mujiks*. My mind boggled at such foolishness, and I admit that he did apologize though with not much humility. He was the kind of man who could make an apology sound far worse than the original insult.

"Yes, I did make a slight error, but no harm has been done. The drug effects soon wear off and you'll both be as right as rain in a moment." I felt like standing up and belting him in the guts but one thing deterred me. He'd replaced the hypodermic syringe in the desk and was holding a stub-nosed revolver.

"Not a political traitor, but a born betrayer, Bill. Any K.G.B. chief who employed you would be sent to Siberia, but I'm more trusting. I'm prepared to employ you, my boy . . . You and dear Peggy." She had come round and Kirk smiled. "I can trust you, because I can rely on *your loyalty*. Under the influence of pentothal you gave a frank account of your career and the facts are even worse than I imagined." He nodded at a cassette recorder on the desk. "Murder . . . blackmail . . . extortion and robbery. Finally concealment of a human corpse. The list is too tedious to be repeated. If one tenth of the charges were preferred you'd be detained at Her Majesty's pleasure for a long time." He clicked his tongue sadly. "A pity to deprive Her Majesty of such *pleasure*, but we must try to save the tax-payer money.

"The confession of your crimes has been fully recorded and the cassette cartridge is in an envelope within my pocket. That envelope is addressed to my solicitor and if he does not hear from me at regular intervals he is instructed to deliver its contents to the proper authorities.

"Taped evidence is not admissible in a court of law, as you are probably aware, but I'm sure the Director of Public Prosecutions will make good use of your admissions."

"Oh, no, Bill, . . . No, Bill, . . . No, Bill, . . . No." I was preparing to make a spring at him, but the little gun came up. "Revolvers are old-fashioned, but far more reliable than automatic weapons and this one is loaded with Dum-Dums. Hollow-nosed bullets, which expand on impact. I don't wish to pull the trigger. The resulting mess would stain my carpet, but I will if necessary . . . Yes, I will."

I was quite certain that he would. Charlie Kirk had made one mistake in imagining we were K.G.B. agents, but he wouldn't make another. The old buzzard had us by the short hairs and I told him so.

"Good. We understand each other, my boy, and I'm prepared to give you a solemn promise. As soon as our mission is completed, I shall tell my solicitor to erase the tape and you will have nothing to fear from the law. I am also prepared to make you a present of the supposed treasure you are seeking." He saw my face light up and chuckled. "The Head of El Dracardo with its diamonds and emeralds has no interest to me. You mentioned Mr Moldon Mott and his purloined relic, but I'm after bigger game.

"As you said, I'm an old man and have no desire for filthy lucre. One head is quite enough, Billy. The head on my shoulders, and it's a downy old head, as you'll learn ere long.

"What do I need in return?" Peggy had questioned him and he nodded at the drinks table. "I'll explain in a moment, though let's have another round first. A more wholesome round this time. I doctored your last noggins with effervescent tablets, but you can play hostess and see there's no hanky-panky, Peggy dear." He spoke as unctuously as Hurst-Hutchins, but it was an act. There was nothing soft or effeminate about the major-general. His brain was as hard and lethal as his revolver.

"Thank you, Peg." She had filled fresh glasses and he leaned under the oil painting again. "I need you because Bill Easter is a completely unscrupulous man and he has had a wide experience of evil.

"Set a thief to catch a thief is a wise maxim, Bill, and that is why your assistance is required. You know about evil and an evil force has possessed this island. A force which I intend to destroy when you've considered these questions." He twirled the revolver between his fingers, but not as a threat; more as a gesture of being threatened.

"What killed James Gordon . . . What is driving the animals mad . . . What exactly are the Ruskis up to?"

The Ruskis . . . The horde of Muscovy. People like Kirk always think there's a Red under every bed and when he told me what he was I understood why.

Before retirement the major-general had been a chief of British Military Intelligence, and being turned out to grass bored him stiff. To while away the idle hours he spent his time slaughtering inoffensive birds when the seasons permitted; pheasants and partridges in Norfolk . . . grouse on Rhona.

But the seasons were too short and the prey too small for the aged warrior. He wanted bigger and more dangerous game and while visiting Rhona he found a worthy quarry. A fat spider was lurking on the island. The spider's name was Comrade Grigory Elfinovich.

Elfinovich . . . I felt that I had heard the name somewhere before, but Kirk didn't elaborate on its owner's identity, though he was a fund of information regarding the comrade's character and achievements. A scientist of note, a senior member of the K.G.B. and a thoroughly bad lot.

So bad, that when Kirk confided his suspicions to the Ministry of Defence, the Minister put him back into harness and gave him *carte blanche* to investigate the mysterious goings-on at Rhona. Hence the respect of Sergeant Gilespie. Hence his suspicions that Peggy and I might be a couple of Soviet agents sent to examine Elfinovich's progress and report on the harvest.

Considerable progress and a distasteful harvest according to Kirk. Its fruit drove the animals mad and Gordon's death suggested that *Homo sapiens* was starting to follow suit. We'd been cleared of killing the pastor because we were wearing shoes. Outside in the garden Kirk had discovered the trail of four naked human feet.

"I don't know what the process is, Bill, but I'm pretty certain why Grigory Elfinovich selected Rhona for his hellish mission." The major-general had prominent white eyebrows and they came up in a bar across his forehead. "In the first place the vegetation is ideal. Belladonna, henbane and the mandrake root are all indigenous to the island and you may have heard what they can do, Peggy."

She hadn't, but I had had a better education. I knew that during the Renaissance several Italian herbalists had produced potions containing the plants he'd mentioned and the effects were similar to those of L.S.D. Dreams and crazed hallucinations leading to a belief that one could fly and become a bird or a beast. Kirk's premise suggested that the mischievous Muscovites had been tampering with the flora of the island . . . hence the behaviour of its fauna.

Possible, I suppose, though I couldn't see why the Russians should have gone to such trouble. I could, however, see one definite flaw. Most of the attacks had been made by dogs and most dogs are carnivorous. They don't eat herbs or raw vegetables.

"A little knowledge is a dangerous thing, Bill." I'd voiced my objections and he hastened to demolish them. "Dogs roll, my boy. They roll in the dirt and they lick themselves clean afterwards. Does that answer your question?"

It answered a small technical point, but I still failed to understand where the Kremlin came in. Why should the Comrade wish to pollute a small and insignificant Scottish island?

"Small . . . yes. Insignificant . . . maybe." He pointed at a map hanging beside his portrait and then moved to a bookcase. "As you can see, Rhona is only a short distance from our rocket bases and there are suggestions that valuable oil deposits may exist beneath the sea bed.

"If the present reign of terror increases, the population is bound to decrease accordingly. Anxiety will lead to panic and there'll be an exodus to the mainland. Rhona will become deserted till fresh settlers move in."

"Sorry, General, but I'm still not with you." I risked a swig of the drink Peg had poured me, and repeated my objections which seemed logical in the extreme.

Granted that the sinister Comrade Grigory Elfinovich had mutated the island's plant life and caused outbreaks of savagery amongst the animals, what good would it do him?

Granted that there was a rush to the mainland, how would the Politburo benefit and who would be the fresh settlers? Even if Rhona became a desert, the island was still part of the United Kingdom and Mrs Thatcher would want to know who those settlers were. If the major-general imagined that a boatload of Soviet tars could row ashore and hoist the red flag he was senile.

"History is not your strong point, Bill, and impertinence does not become you." Kirk pulled a leather-bound volume out of the case, but still kept his revolver pointing in my direction. "The Island of Rhona may cease to be part of the United Kingdom and I'll tell you why." He laid the book on the table and fitted a pince-nez to the bridge of his nose. "Since the Middle Ages, the Stuart-Vail family have ruled Rhona like feudal overlords, and Lady Elizabeth has the legal right to cancel her allegiance to the British Realm.

"During the Jacobite Rebellion of seventeen forty five the

reigning laird, Sir Douglas Vail, refused to throw in his lot with Bonnie Prince Charlie and remained loyal to the House of Hanover." Kirk thumbed through the pages while he spoke. "A misplaced loyalty in my opinion, but Sir Douglas reaped his reward. The Duke of Cumberland, Butcher Cumberland or Stinking Billy, as the Scots still call him, made Sir Douglas a promise. If Rhona was held for the crown, the crown would express its gratitude.

"Rhona was held and after Prince Charles was defeated at Culloden, the House of Hanover honoured Cumberland's promise. In seventeen forty six, King George the Third and the English Parliament sent Sir Douglas an insane agreement which runs as follows." He had found the reference he wanted and read aloud.

"In view of patents supplied by our devoted servant and victorious general, William Augustus Duke of Cumberland, we . . ."

"Oh, I can't be bothered with the legal jargon, Bill." Kirk pulled off his pince-nez and let it dangle from a cord around his neck. "An insane proposition, as I said, but all the early Georges were insane. They were also cursed with a malicious sense of humour. The King obviously imagined that the promises would be revoked by his heirs and never kept.

"But they haven't been revoked, my friends, and the conditions are still binding." He closed the book and reached for his cigar which was smouldering in an ash-tray.

"As long as twenty Christian families are residing on Rhona, the island will remain subject to the crown of Great Britain. Should the population fall below that number, however, complete independence shall be granted and all titles and rights transferred to Sir Douglas Vail (the Stuart was added much later), his descendants and assigns.

"That edict is still on the statute book, Bill, and if Elfinovich's hellish plot succeeds the population may drop below the stipulated figure and we could have a Russian base on this island."

"I'm not saying that Lady Elizabeth would make the transfer freely, of course, but she may have been deprived of her freedom. My belief is that Elfinovich and his henchmen are holding the Stuart-Vails captive in the castle. That they have been brainwashed.

That as soon as the population falls below the allotted figure, Lady Elizabeth will sign whatever Grigory Elfinovich tells her to sign.

"A frightening prospect, but with the help of God and William Easter we will avoid it." He looked at his watch and motioned us to stand up. "I'll explain more on the way to Drabster, and we must make our way there. The evening ferry leaves in half an hour and takes the mail with it. The recording of your misdeeds goes with that mail, Billy boy, and I'll outline your instructions in the car." He wound a muffler around his neck and moved towards the door.

"Don't look so glum, Billy. You came to Rhona to reclaim a treasure and I'm prepared to help you. All I want is one small service in return. Enter the castle and report on everything you see there."

"No, I must be frank and two services could be required." He laid a hand on the door knob and then paused. "If the worst comes to the worst you will have to kill Comrade Grigory Elfinovich."

Why me? If the situation was so desperate, why didn't Kirk summon the experts? The S.A.S., the Marine Commandos, the Brigade of Guards? Even Sergeant Gilespie and the local Boy Scouts would have been a better bet and I told him so.

"Much better, but my hands are tied at the moment." The general spoke figuratively, because his hands weren't tied. He'd ordered me to take the wheel and was lolling in the back seat with Peggy. Through the driving mirror I could see that his hands were free and one of 'em was in his pocket with the revolver to keep it company.

"Though I would naturally prefer to employ professionals, an Englishman's home is his castle and the same applies to a Scotswoman's residence.

"There is no doubt that Inverlee Castle is occupied by a group of Bolshevik agents, but I can hardly send in the troops without proof, which you must obtain."

"Lady Elizabeth and her relatives have almost certainly been brainwashed by their captors and are co-operating with them, and there is also the question of the bailiff and his wife.

"You know about Allan Grant, Bill?" He nodded when I used

the name. "The Grants are difficult characters to understand, and I still have difficulty in summing them up.

"Allan's family have worked for the Stuart-Vails for nine generations and Molly's term of servitude is almost as long. On the surface two devoted and loyal retainers . . . Beneath the surface . . ." He paused and shrugged. "I think that Molly may be the stronger of the two and she's certainly the more intelligent, which caused the trouble.

"Intelligence is no recommendation for an under-parlourmaid, but the last male laird, Lady Elizabeth's father, didn't share my view.

"He sent Molly to Glasgow University and the London School of Economics." Kirk made the institutions sound like Sodom and Gomorrah. "That's probably how the rot started. Molly had a taste of Communist doctrines and they festered when she returned to the island.

"Mere supposition, of course, but I'm pretty certain that Comrade Elfinovich did not arrive here by accident. He was invited to Rhona and the Grants issued the invitation.

"Brainwashing and loyalty turned sour, Bill. The Stuart-Vails are under the thumb of Grigory Elfinovich, and so are their minions.

"That's why I can't order troops to raid the castle, but you'll do the job just as well. A Trojan horse within the gates, a professional criminal after plunder.

"You can take your plunder with my blessing, Bill, but you must give me a full report on what is going on inside the castle and take pictures. You also have *carte blanche* to kill Elfinovich and anyone else who tries to stop you.

"Don't quibble, my boy." I'd merely asked how I could take pictures of, or kill an armed Russian thug, without a camera or a gun, but the enquiry irritated him. "You'll have all the equipment and information you need and I'm relying on your cunning.

"You believe that that South American trophy is worth a million pounds sterling and you'll earn it. You will also have the chance to serve your country, though I don't suppose that counts for much.

"The tape recording of your misdeeds counts a great deal,

however, so draw up on the left and I'll place it in safe keeping."

We had reached the quay and I saw that the ferry boat was alongside with passengers filing up the gangway. I stopped the car obediently and not on account of old Kirk's revolver. I was perfectly willing to play ball with him if it earned me Dracardo's head and I wasn't worried about his cassette tape. He himself had said that recorded evidence was not admissible, and I felt pretty certain that the envelope would never reach the Public Prosecutor.

Not out of Christian charity, of course. The major-general lacked in that quality, but he valued his good name. A name which would stink to heaven if the authorities did decide to take action. Obtaining a confession from a man under the influence of a noxious foreign drug. Not cricket . . . Not British . . . Poor sportsmanship. No jury would listen to the tape and General Charlie would be blackballed by every club in London.

I didn't tell him that of course. I watched him climb out and pop his package into a letter box. I made a mental list of my requirements while he sauntered back to the car. I considered the name Comrade Grigory Elfinovich. I knew who its owner really was or rather had been.

"And now we must return the sergeant's car and prepare for your mission, Bill. A dangerous mission, but I'm sure you'll do your duty for Queen and Country." He chuckled wheezily as I drove on. "My spy will enter Jericho and there'll be no Rahab, the Harlot, to shelter him."

Fourteen

Rahab the Harlot . . . Kirk the Contemptible. A cowardly conniver who was blackmailing me into doing a dirty job which should have been left to the specialists.

The Bible tells us that Rahab was a lady of easy virtue who shielded two of Joshua's spies when they entered Jericho to prepare for the Israelite assault. As soon as Joshua was ready, Rahab lowered the agents to safety on a rope, the trumpets blew and the Lord of Hosts demolished Jericho's defences.

That is according to Holy Writ, but I believe that the city fell for a more practical reason.

The crafty invaders undermined Jericho and propped up their tunnels with timber soaked in turpentine or some such inflammable substance. The props were ignited, the walls crumbled once fire consumed their temporary foundation and it was then that the trumpets sounded and the Children of Israel advanced.

An interesting piece of history, but it didn't provide me with comfort. Charlie Kirk had admitted that I'd find no companionable Rahab inside Inverlee Castle, he wasn't in touch with Jehovah, and he couldn't imitate Joshua and dig mines. A survey map and a set of architect's drawings in Gilespie's office showed that the building was surrounded by a ridge of granite.

I had to enter the castle alone and in the teeth of Comrade Elfinovich and his Bolshevik thugs, his fellow-travellers, Allan Grant and his wife, and the brain-washed Stuart-Vails.

A daunting prospect, but the thought of Dracardo's head made the risks worthwhile, and I'm not subject to despair. Kirk wanted me to spy out the land so that he could sound his own trumpet for the S.A.S. to charge in, and I might be prepared to help him if I bumped into the sinister Comrades. But first things come first and Mott's purloined treasure was my top priority. Once I had the loot, Grigory Elfinovich would cease to concern me.

The castle grounds were open to the public between two and six the next day and Peggy and I promised to meet Kirk outside them at three o'clock sharp. In return he promised to supply the items I required for the mission and bring them along with him.

Promised rather reluctantly, though he couldn't refuse. I still played the felon under duress, but the major-general realized that he had to scratch my back if I was to reciprocate. We were partners, reluctant bedfellows and every successful business venture is based on goodwill.

A set of locksmith's tools . . . A pistol . . . A pocket compass . . . a miner's helmet fitted with a torch. An aerosol spray of nerve gas and a breathing mask to protect the sprayer. I knew that the boffins had produced stuff which can knock a man cold in seconds. I also wanted a metal detector and a few other items and he went to a telephone and contacted an army base on the mainland. I looked at Gilespie's map and the architect's drawings.

I must have spent half an hour studying the terrain, and I'm blessed with a keen eye for architectural detail. By the time I'd finished and Kirk had ordered his stores I was pretty sure I could walk through most of Inverlee Castle blindfolded, though I stress the word *most*.

The existing structure is a pretentious nineteenth-century residence, but though the house had been completed in 1878, it stood upon the foundations of a far older building and the plans didn't help. Information was obtainable from a horse's mouth, however. I questioned Kirk, Kirk questioned Gilespie and the sergeant hurried away and returned with an aged rustic who tottered into the office leaning on a stick.

I think Gilespie introduced him as Alexander Selkirk, which seemed unlikely, but his surname didn't matter. What mattered was that Alexander was not only a keen archaeologist. He had been employed at the castle in several capacities since he was a lad. Knife boy to footman . . . Footman to gillie . . . Gillie to chauffeur when infirmity relegated him from the copse to a chassis. He had now been pensioned off and lived with his wedded daughter. A grasping, ill-tempered female in Alexander's view. She had four children and would probably have sent him to an old folks' home if he *hadn't got a bit put by.* She obviously had no time to listen to her parent's chatter and he liked to chatter. In particular he liked to talk about his past.

He didn't enquire why I wanted to know about the castle foundations. He didn't care. He just wanted to talk, and the foundations were as good a subject as any. He propped up his stick, creaked into a chair and opened his toothless gums.

Mr Selkirk, or whatever his name was, talked for far longer than the half-hour I'd spent studying the plans and much of his lecture was worthless servants' hall reminiscing.

How he'd tumbled a housemaid on the laird's *ain* bed. How he'd caught a poacher in Glen Garren. How he and another fun-loving lad had fixed a cord across the stairs which brought the butler crashing to the feet of a visiting prime minister.

Kirk and I had to prod and guide him along the path to knowledge, but though my head was reeling before he came to the point I finally got what I wanted.

The original castle was a medieval keep. The foundations which remained had formed the dungeons of the keep and they'd been well-occupied in days of yore. The Vail family (Stuart was only added during the last century), as Kirk said, were constantly at loggerheads with rival clans and fortune usually smiled on them. A full house was kept beneath the castle walls and some of the guests remained there. Alexander had seen their skeletons.

The main door to the dungeons was bolted and barred, but he and his mate with the trip cord had discovered another entrance. The stream from Saint Freda's shrine disappeared underground after leaving the pool, but that hadn't deterred the bold Alexander. The two lads had climbed down and ended up in the jail house. They'd made a full tour of the dungeons and he recounted what they'd seen with a wealth of gruesome detail.

But he had also done something else which made my spirits soar. The dotard must have possessed the gift of the gab since he learned to speak and when he was a young man he'd confided his discoveries to her present Leddyship's half-brother.

"To Maister Oliver Hendricks . . . Him what became an English clergyman . . . Him they say killed them women." His tone suggested that joining the C. of E. was a greater evil than murder, but I wasn't interested in doctrinal disputes. I wanted to know about Oliver Hendricks and the knowledge was forthcoming.

All boys like secret places and Oliver had been shown an underground kingdom which he regarded as his own. The dungeons obsessed him and hardly a day passed when he didn't crawl down the stream to his domain.

An unhealthy obsession in Alexander's opinion. "Nae canny . . . a wee grue . . . a bit fey," were three of the expressions he used and my elation increased.

The child's the father of the man and where would a man conceal a treasure? In a boyhood hidey-hole, of course, and to hell with Charles Kirk and Comrade Grigory Elfinovich. I wasn't going to prowl around the house and get entangled with a bunch of

Russians. Whether the general liked it or not, the S.A.S. were the lads for that work. I'd visit the grounds as arranged. I'd hang about till the last tourist left and lie low in a disused stable Kirk had told me about. But, after that the arrangements would change. There was no need to go near the castle itself. The head was somewhere in the stream or in the dungeons unless the gipsy woman Gordon spotted had made off with it, which seemed unlikely to me in my present state of euphoria.

"You're welcome to anything you find, Bill, but duty comes first." Kirk shared Peggy's mind reading abilities and demonstrated them again. "I want a full report on what's going on at Inverlee Castle with particular reference to this man." He held out a photograph for my inspection. "That is Mr Elfinovich, and he shouldn't be difficult to recognize."

He was quite right. The face on the print was an ordinary, almost an anonymous face but lacked one appendage; a left ear. Either the comrade had been born without the organ or someone had sliced it off.

"Yes, easily identifiable, but proof of identity is required." Kirk took the picture from me and slipped something into my hand. A blue pebble set in a silver surround with what looked like hieroglyphics carved on the metal. "A talisman for your protection, Bill. A cairngorm brooch which signifies that you are a member of the Stuart-Vail clan. Also a gadget to protect you from me. Press the catch, please. Press it just once. Microfilm is hard to come by and there are only five shots on the reel.

"Yes, a camera, Bill." I'd flicked the pin and seen a shutter open and close in the centre of the stone. "When your task is accomplished I shall expect to receive another photograph of our quarry. The man without an ear.

"And don't . . . don't imagine you can play me false, my boy." He moved to a window and nodded at a fishing boat out to sea. "That is a naval vessel and there are several more in the vicinity. Their captains have orders to search every unauthorized craft approaching or leaving Rhona.

"You can't get off the island without my permission, Bill, and I shall take another precaution. While you're at work, tomorrow afternoon, Peggy will stay with me as a hostage for your good behaviour."

Indeed! Really! How very clever of the major-general! I tried to look impressed, but he'd given me the final fillip. I'd get off the island despite his naval flotilla and I'd wanted to be rid of Peggy for a long time. Charlie was welcome to Mrs Maggie Tey and if I'd had a drink I'd have raised the glass to Rudyard Kipling.

"The serf in the field or the king on the throne,
He travels the fastest who travels alone."

I intended to travel fast, but I wouldn't be lonely. The Dracardo head would keep me company.

That concluded our business, and we arranged to meet Kirk at 3 o'clock outside the castle next day. He promised to bring the equipment I'd asked for with him and I promised to be on time and ready to face the Russian steam-roller.

We parted company and the next twenty-four hours passed uneventfully, though I had a piece of business of my own to transact; arrangements for the getaway, and I honestly believe that God guided my hand. He certainly guided our feet to the Thistle Inn for a quick dram before going to bed and the drams were paid for by Dan and Fergus Bryde who were now on the best of terms with little Tony Cayne. The doctor's evil reputation had been erased and the cup of kindness was flowing. Mrs Alison, the taciturn lady behind the bar, was also more cheerful. Probably because business was brisk and the room was crammed with hearty characters looking forward to the morra.

When I asked what the morra would bring, Fergus called me an ignorant Sassenach. Tomorrow was the twelfth of course. The glorious twelfth of August when the grouse shooting season began and a public holiday on Rhona.

A disturbing piece of news. I wanted to make my departure peacefully, but the hills would be dotted with trigger-happy sportsmen blazing away at the birds. They might easily blaze at me when I crossed their line of fire, and I told Peggy to telephone

Kirk and say that our meeting must be postponed till five when the barrage subsided.

While she was getting through and talking to Kirk, I noticed one individual who didn't appear to be a sportsman and certainly didn't look cheerful. A gaunt figure in a shabby blue uniform sitting at the counter. The Brydes informed me that he was a skipper of a salvage tug and had no reason to cheer. His vessel had abandoned a valuable prize owing to engine trouble and put in to Drabster for temporary repairs. She was due to limp back to the Clyde tomorrow night however, so I approached the distressed mariner and enquired whether he'd take a passenger with him.

He would for a few pence and I followed him into the Gents. The few pence turned out to be thirty pounds, but he asked no tiresome questions and made only one stipulation. His boat, the *Winsome Jean*, would sail on the evening tide and tide, like time, waits for no man. If I wasn't on board by seven o'clock he'd go without me. I handed over three tenners and we shook hands on the bargain.

That was that. Peggy had spoken to Kirk who had reluctantly agreed to the postponement, and we returned to the *Pension Mackenzie* and went to bed.

But I couldn't sleep. I thought what the next day might bring. Death at the hands of Comrade Grigory Elfinovich. Freedom from Mrs Margaret Tey with a crock of gold to comfort me. I felt quite certain that Mott's treasure was in Saint Freda's stream or down in the castle dungeons and I knew how to get into the dungeons and out again. I had arranged my escape route and the *Winsome Jean* would carry me over the sea from Rhona. Given a fraction of luck I'd have sold my trophy and be a rich man before the week was out and I hummed the same shanty I'd sung in Smeaton's basement.

"Beyond the Chagres River, they say,
The story's old.
Lie paths that lead to mountains
Of purest virgin gold."

A tempting ditty, but I couldn't remember the last verse, though I remembered something else when I climbed out of bed and closed the window. The damned dogs were giving tongue again. A hellish chorus of howls and bellows and insane yelps which jogged my memory and aroused my suspicions.

General Charlie Kirk thought he had me under his thumb, so why had he lied? There might be a nest of Soviet agents in Inverlee Castle but their leader could hardly be called Grigory Elfinovich.

The owner of that name had been murdered in 1916, though he'd taken a deal of killing. He drank two glasses of poisoned wine and then offered to take his murderers to a brothel. He was shot three times and one bullet pierced his heart. He stood up and battered down a locked door. His skull was split by a club, but that didn't kill him. He was still breathing when he was tied up in a blanket and thrown under the ice of a river. When his body was found he had released the ropes, and some people said that it was not his body.

How could the *Starets* die? Who could kill the Healer? The Holy Man of Christ . . . The Saviour, and the Destroyer? Grigory Elfinovich Rasputin . . . Mad Monk of Russia?

Fifteen

"You're late." Peggy and Kirk had gone ahead in a police car. I'd followed by bus in the interests of secrecy and the general scowled at his watch when I alighted outside the castle. "Twenty minutes late and the grounds close at six sharp." His scowl darkened though I couldn't see how he could blame me. I was late because the bus was late. It had kept stopping because the grouse shooters were blazing across the road and the driver hadn't even honked his horn at them.

"No excuse . . . No time for excuses." Kirk climbed out of the car and heaved a rucksack after him. "All the equipment you asked for is in there, though I couldn't get a miner's helmet and you won't need one. I'll expect you out of the house long before sunset and that's the only important item." His tone softened as he saw the camera brooch pinned to my lapel. "And if you don't get out, Bill, we'll know that Elfinovich has captured you and an

S.A.S. unit is ready to storm the castle tomorrow."

"You'll be all right darling, and so will I." Peggy's eyes glowed with mock concern and obvious greed. "If you get killed General Kirk's promised that I can have the treasure, so you needn't worry about me."

I wasn't worried about her. I was just astonished by the extent of her cupidity, but Kirk didn't give me a chance to say so.

"Bill won't be killed, my dear. South Americans, West Africans and cockney gangsters couldn't kill Billy Easter, and I'm sure Comrade Grigory Elfinovich will be equally unsuccessful.

"I have faith in your powers of survival, dear boy, and you've got the tools for survival. A nerve gas spray, a set of lock picks and I've even included my revolver for good measure. You've got all you need, but have you got a florin?"

"A florin?" I hadn't heard the term for years and didn't know what he meant at first. "Whatever for?"

"For that fellow." He pointed at a kilted figure by the gate. "The price of admission is one florin or ten new pence in modern parlance and Allan Grant was a Regimental Sergeant Major of the Argylls. He demands the exact sum, so have you got a florin?"

Why an R.S.M. of the Argylls or any other unit shouldn't dole out change was beyond me, but I assured Kirk that I had plenty of ten p pieces available.

"Good." His pointing finger moved towards a cluster of outhouses at the back of the main building. "Those are the stables where you will hide and Peggy and I had better go first. If you should happen to be captured we don't want to be associated with you till the army takes over.

"Right." Just *right*. No loving kiss from Peg. No manly handshake from Kirk. He took her arm and they strolled off as though preparing to board a train. A callous old man, with a callous middle-aged woman at his side.

I had to face terrible dangers, but they didn't care, and only the thought of the future kept me cheerful. Mott's golden orb in the haversack and the *Winsome Jean* bearing me to Glasgow. Kirk and Peggy expected me back before sunset, but I'd be hell and gone with the evening tide.

I slung the pack over my shoulder and waited for Kirk to present the gate-keeper with the exact fee.

"Thank you, sir." Allan Grant tucked my ten pence into his sporran, and attempted to smile. An attempt which failed. Apart from a lantern jaw and sunken cheeks, his eyes were as hard as the pebble in my brooch. They were also troubled eyes, though I didn't look at them long. My role was that of an ordinary day-tripper eager to view the places of interest and I gave him another florin and received a leaflet describing those places.

The Gallows . . . The Stocks . . . The Flogging Tree . . . The Seat of Repentance . . . Traitors' Leap. Apart from some lovely scenery, Inverlee Castle hadn't much to attract tourists unless they were sado-masochists or students of corporal punishment.

Traitors' Leap; a hundred-foot cliff from which the Stuart-Vails' opponents had been hurled to their doom, had a fine view of the Atlantic, but most of the exhibits were replicas to create amusement and swell the family's coffers. The stocks and the gallows were obviously of modern construction, though the Seat of Repentance might be original. A metal stool with rows of spikes intended to discomfort the sitter. The spikes had corroded over the years however, and I saw Peggy lower her rump on 'em and giggle.

Pipe music was swirling out from a loudspeaker, but the tunes were interrupted by bangs and whoops in the hills above. For a moment I imagined the dogs were giving tongue again, but I was wrong. A human pack was on the rampage. Beaters driving the grouse to their slaughterers.

There weren't many other visitors and I noticed that the curtains of the house were tightly drawn. Possibly because Comrade Elfinovich and his gang of Soviet agents were in occupation, though I doubted that. Grigory Elfinovich was a product of Kirk's senile imagination. The old boy had invented the yarn to get back between the shafts and feel important. Balls to the Bolsheviks and a raspberry for Rasputin.

The curtains were drawn because the family were distressed by Oliver Hendricks' deprecations and they didn't want a crowd of tourists gaping at them. The animal hysteria could be accounted for by an abnormally rich henbane harvest. Two perfectly simple explanations, and my own task appeared equally simple. Get into the shrine . . . Climb down the stream to the dungeons and grab the reward.

Kirk had told me to play the role of an innocent visitor and I acted accordingly. I looked at the Leap, I examined the stocks and the gallows. I was strolling towards the stables he'd mentioned when I stopped strolling. I belted into the nearest outhouse like a drunk trying to reach a pub before closing time and slammed the door behind me. I peered through a gap in the woodwork and prayed that my eyes had deceived me.

No mistake . . . no deception. A fierce gingery figure was standing beside the Flogging Tree and looking as though he wished he had a whip in his hand and a back to play it on.

J. Moldon Mott had arrived to make sure I kept our bargain and retrieved his property.

Kirk had said that the grounds closed at six and as the castle clock started to strike the hour, the pipe music was replaced by the hectoring tone of Allan Grant.

"Out . . . All visitors will now leave." I say hectoring, and I was right. The ex-R.S.M. had doubtless scared the daylights out of a thousand raw recruits, but there was also a plea in his voice too which didn't match the orders. Grant sounded as though he was desperate to get rid of his guests, and most of them obeyed and filed away with Kirk and Peg leading the exodus.

I was alone, but I didn't leave the stable for a while. I checked the contents of the bag Kirk had given me. Apart from the miner's lamp, the items were all present and correct, though I wished I'd asked him to provide a rope and a pair of climbing boots for my descent down the stream. However the ancient warrior didn't know I was going via the stream and you can't prepare for everything. At least he popped in a hand torch which should be sufficient.

I closed the rucksack, had another peer through the gap in the door and saw that the coast was clear, though the sounds of the hunters still rumbled from the hills. I also saw the exit which

I'd hoped to see. Like Mr Gordon's manse the garden wall was covered by azalea bushes, but fifty yards from the stable there was a wicket gate with a track winding up through the bracken and heather. A track to Saint Freda's well. The route to my treasure.

The shrine was as the Rev. Gordon had described it. A shallow cave beneath a crag and a pool fed by a stream from the slopes above. I didn't see any traces of a dead rabbit or a cloaked lady, however, and I hadn't really expected to. Like the boys from Muscovy and Comrade Rasputin, Lilith, the Mother of Evil, was another product of the imagination. Jimmy Gordon might have surprised a gipsy woman though. A woman clutching a yellow football . . . the orb . . . Dracardo's Head . . . the future.

The tunnel leading down from the pool would probably have been impassable in the winter, and the recent rain still made the climb difficult, though not unduly difficult. I decided to make the descent in my socks, however, and took off my shoes. The journey would be uncomfortable, but better to graze a foot than slip and break my spine. I eased myself through the crack in the rocks and set off.

The journey was uncomfortable and difficult and my main enemy was the dark. I cursed Kirk for not supplying a miner's lantern, because his torch was useless. I needed both hands to grip the rocks which were jagged and slippery. I almost twisted an ankle and I cracked my head on the roof of the channel twice.

I was bleeding and soaked and blind in the darkness when the route suddenly levelled and my fingers clutched something which wasn't rock and felt soft and flabby. I pulled out the pocket torch and saw what it was. The rusty remains of a door which had once secured the dungeons. A single shove pushed the frame aside and I was half-way home, though certainly not home and dry. My clothes were dripping, my head was throbbing from the impacts, and I could hardly believe my eyes when I stepped into the Stuart-Vails' subterranean Dartmoor.

A horrible penitentiary. As horrible as Allen Smeaton's basement and still occupied, though the occupants bore no resemblance to his bloated tenant. At least a dozen skeletons were hanging from the wall facing me and they'd been dead for centuries. I didn't count the exact number and I wasn't interested. I'd expected the corpses because Alexander Selkirk had said that they were there and I had no reason to doubt his story.

But there was one cadaver I had not expected and it wasn't a skeleton and it wasn't chained against the wall. The body lay on the floor and it was clad in what appeared to have been a dressing-gown and a pair of pyjamas. The body of a middle-aged man who might have been Kirk's imaginary Grigory Elfinovich because he certainly lacked an ear. The poor sod also lacked a nose and a mouth and a throat and he hadn't really got a face.

The historical Rasputin had died in 1916, but Kirk's invention had died more recently according to the date on his wrist watch which had stopped three months ago. He looked as though he had been torn by a machine, and I drew back from him quickly.

Too quickly. Something caught the side of my head and for the third time since landing on Rhona I was knocked cold.

The object I'd collided against was innocent enough. The figure of another man, but a hollow man. A suit of armour which had been placed in the dungeons as a symbol of *Abandon Hope, All Ye Who Enter Here*. If I'd been wearing shoes I'd probably have given the effigy a kick in his breastplate, but when my senses returned hope soared.

The martial image had been knocked over during the impact and it lay beside me with its visor open. My torch was still functioning and I saw that, though the rest of the suit was empty, the head-piece was not. Behind the steel slot, a brighter metal glinted and I knew that I really was home at last.

The helmet was only attached to the rest of the suit by clamps and a twist loosened it. I didn't know how the head itself could be loosened, but I'd cross that bridge later. The golden head was inside the steel head and I'd got what I wanted. My hunch and information had paid dividends and all that remained was to pack up my treasure and make off. Off to fresh woods and pastures new and I didn't give the chap in the dressing-gown a second thought. Dead Soviet agents were no concern of mine. My concern was Number

One and I unzipped Kirk's rucksack and dumped the contents on the floor. There was just enough room for the helmet, though it was a heavy burden which jarred my spine as I slung the pack over my shoulder, but that didn't bother me. I was Hercules . . . Atlas bearing the world on my back and all I had to do was to get back. Back up the stream . . . Back across the brass and the bracken . . . Back to Drabster and then all aboard the *Skylark*.

"What do I care if the parents pine,
For once aboard the lugger and the girl is mine."

I sang loudly and cheerfully, and I didn't give a damn who pined. Peggy and Kirk and J. Moldon Mott could pine to their hearts' content. Dracardo's head was my property and Mott had valued it at a million pounds. If I couldn't find a buyer I deserved to spend the rest of my life on public assistance and my financial worries were over.

". . . Once aboard the lugger and the girl is mine."

I don't know how long my elation lasted, but I know how suddenly it stopped, though I'm not sure why. Like the Rev. Jimmy Gordon I didn't hear or see anything and nor did I smell anything. But I sensed something and I crept towards the stream, trying to pretend that I wasn't afraid, which wasn't true. I was bloody terrified and there's a vast difference between fear and terror.

Comrade Elfinovich had died recently and his companions centuries ago. They couldn't hurt me, but other forces might, though I had no idea what the forces were. I just knew that I wasn't alone in the dungeons and I had to get out.

When Mott sent his wolves down to Smeaton's basement, he explained that animals possess an inborn sense that modern man has lost. I am a product of the twentieth century, but my sense of danger was as loud as an alarm bell. Someone or something was watching me and that thing had a brain . . . an evil intelligence which bore me no goodwill. The time for stealth and pretence was over and I bolted for the exit like a rat to his hole.

But I couldn't make the journey . . . Not with the pack on my shoulders. The roof of the tunnel was too low and the walls too narrow. The rocks tore at the haversack, their grip tightened at every yard, while the thing behind drew closer. A thing which I couldn't face and there was only one course of action. An act which I've never regretted, though it cost me a fortune. I released the harness and abandoned my burden. The rucksack and its contents went bumping down the slope, but I didn't care. I was free and could climb on without hindrance. Let the Devil keep his own. Billy Easter had kept his sanity.

I was still terrified when I left the stream, and I didn't stop for my shoes. My intuitive sense of evil remained and not only intuition made me stumble on. A rank, pungent smell was drifting up through the tunnel and I had to breathe fresh air or be suffocated. I had to keep running or go mad, and I did run. I ran away from the shrine till my feet slipped and I fell gasping against a tussock and praying to God, the Deliverer.

My prayers continued for about three minutes before I realized that I had allies. God's guardian angels were hard at work delivering me.

Two old, grey-muzzled sheep dogs were stationed by the entrance of the cave. Their hackles were up, their bodies quivered with anger, their jaws gaped, but they didn't bark.

They just growled. Deep, snarling growls full of menace and fury.

My protectors stopped snarling after a while. Whatever had aroused their wrath appeared to have beat a retreat. Panic stations were over and they left the cave and turned their attention to me.

I'd thought of 'em as guardian angels, but I was wrong. They were rozzers and gamekeepers and I'd been caught trespassing. I had to give an account of my actions or go along to the police station.

Though old and grey, the leader of the pair was obviously as spry as Kirk and had an impressive set of yellow teeth. His companion was also old, but extremely large for a collie. Almost as large as one of Mott's timber wolves and equally formidable. I didn't like the look of either of 'em and remembered what I'd heard about the sheep killing and other cases of savagery. I looked for a stone to lob at them but changed my mind when they sidled towards me. I wasn't dealing with fools. These were professionals who knew their trade. One would have my right hand between his fangs while t'other was attending to my throat. Submission was the only course, so I tried the soft word which is supposed to turn away wrath.

"Hullo, boy. There's a good doggie." A civil enough greeting but it didn't turn away wrath. The words raised a wrathful bark with a clear meaning.

"Stand up . . . Cause no trouble and we might . . . just *might* see that you get off lightly."

I did stand up because I've heard such orders before and usually found it better to obey them. I had no idea what the canine policemen had seen or smelled in the cave, but I knew they'd take a dim view of insubordination. I held out my left fist for the leader to sniff and show that I meant no harm, but the gesture was ignored. He stalked away three paces and then turned and gave another gruff command. His companion growled at my heels and there was no doubt that I was under arrest. I decided to play ball and follow the leader.

The trouble was that the leader was a difficult chap to follow and the rear escort had a nasty nature. They were trained to work sheep and appeared to imagine I was a stray from their flock. I used to enjoy watching the sheep dog trials on television, but have never looked at one again.

Over hill and dale . . . across streams and dry stone walls, through a bog and down a scree shock. My stockinged feet were bleeding after a hundred yards, but a cracking pace was maintained. Any hesitation caused the vanguard's displeasure and more than once the lad in the rear took a nip at my ankles. As we pounded along I seemed to hear the jovial tones of Mr Drabble, the television commentator, reporting progress. "Oh, there's no doubt that those old dogs know their business. A most experienced couple of collies and driving hard all the way. Under complete control and not a point lost."

Driving hard and driving far. I'd been exhausted when I climbed out of the stream. I was tottering before the end of the journey. My lungs seemed to be bursting when I staggered against a gate post and knew I could run no further. I leaned on the gate and waited for the arresting officers to show their displeasure.

They may have been displeased, but they didn't show displeasure. I heard no growls or baring of teeth. I heard voices.

"Stop that, Grip. What the hell are you up to, Grapple?" the first voice said. "Down this instant, the pair of you, and leave the gentleman be," said the second. Both voices were rough and uncouth, but they were the most beautiful voices I'd ever heard and my persecutors slunk away. Dogs can tell when a person is afraid of them and I'd been afraid when they first met me. I was sweating with terror and the odour of adrenalin must have aroused their indignation. But the tones of uneducated command soon reminded them that man is the ruler of the brute creation and one brute received a touch of his ruler's stick in reward for self-righteousness. "Hie away to the barn," said the first voice. "Why if it isn't Mr Easter?" enquired the second, and then a third issued an invitation.

"Come and join our party," said Dr Tony Cayne.

Sixteen

Party! To show that Tony Cayne was cleared of demonology and to celebrate the start of the grouse season Dan and Fergus Bryde had invited the doctor to their farm and a drunken revel was in progress. Several other friends, including Alexander Selkirk and his wedded daughter, were present and good fellowship was the order of the day. Alex's daughter treated my feet and legs with disinfectant she said was used to scrub out cow byres, and stung like hell. Dan lent me a pair of shoes which didn't fit but were better than nothing. Fergus handed me a tumbler of colourless liquid to restore my strength. Imagining it was water, I swallowed the contents in one gulp and then choked. Whisky . . . neat malt whisky! Many of the island whiskys are colourless and *Rhona Dew* is one of 'em. I'd knocked back a quarter of a bottle and it burned like acid.

My discomfort raised a roar of merriment till I was helped into a deck chair and recounted what I'd experienced. If my audience had been English rustics they'd have probably been sceptical about my premonitions of evil, but these were Highland Scots and as superstitious as they come. The whole bunch fell silent for a moment and then Fergus whistled his dogs and rewarded them with a couple of marrow bones. He considered that Grip and Grapple were the heroes of the hour. They had known that something uncanny had followed me up into Freda's shrine and being trusty friends they'd driven me over the hills to safety.

A view I didn't share. In my opinion the collies had been motivated by the insolence of office, but I didn't express my doubts. I showed my gratitude by patting Grip and scratching Grapple's brindled scalp. Courtesy costs nothing and the dogs might have sensed a hostile force in the shrine.

"There's nowt uncanny in them dungeons." The only doubter was old Selkirk and he questioned me more closely. "Why did you go down there and what boggle did you really see, Mr Easter?"

I couldn't tell him the reasons for my visit, and I hadn't actually seen any boggle. I adopted the same attitude I'd used in the Thistle Inn. Business connected with the recent unfortunate events on Rhona. Can't say any more on account of the Official Secrets Act, but he could take my word that there were some very obnoxious skeletons in the dungeon cupboards.

"Of course there are skeletons and they've been there for hundreds of years." Alex was still unimpressed. He appeared to regard the stream and the dungeons as his own domain full of happy boyhood memories. "But corpses can't harm one and I'll prove it.

"You say that yer lost yer haversack, Mr Easter, and it's near the bottom of the stream packed with equipment." He straightened and raised his stick. "You're too scared to go back for your equipment, but Alexander Selkirk's not scared. I may be old and a bit unsteady on me pins, but there's nothing wrong with me arms or courage."

"You mean that you'll climb down and fetch the pack for me, Mr Selkirk?" Serious thinking was needed and I accepted another small glass of Rhona Dew to gain time. Even the golden head wouldn't persuade me to set foot in that hellish cavern again, but I wanted the head very badly. If someone could retrieve the ruck-sack for me I'd be duly grateful, but what if the someone stumbled on Comrade Elfinovich's corpse at the same time. A gamble or a calculated risk? I asked Fergus to dilute his fire water with a little tap water and considered the position . . . the position of the body. The suit of armour had fallen between the dead comrade and the prison entrance and it was unlikely that Alexander would notice the body. Whatever he might say, there was something uncanny lurking in the gloom and he'd grab my pack and beat a hasty retreat. Or rather be hauled up with a rope to speed his exit.

I looked at him critically and saw that he was skinny enough to pass through the tunnel with the pack on his shoulders, and judging by the wedded daughter's expression he wouldn't be greatly missed if the boggles got him.

"Of course Father will fetch your belongings, sir." It was the daughter who made the decision. "He's spry enough for his years and he knows the place like the back of his hand. Always talking about them dratted caverns and I'm sick of the sound of them."

"Shut yer mouth, Flora." The old fool brandished the stick at her. "There's twenty thousand pounds of mine in the Scottish Linen Bank and it'll go to charity if there's any more of your inso-lence.

"Aye, Alexander Selkirk's got money and he's got the strength and courage, Mr Easter. I'm feared of no man and no boggle can harm me."

"Then prove your courage." Daughter Flora ignored the stick and issued a challenge which was echoed by the trolls and their guests. Most people respect bravery and despise bravado, and Selkirk was clearly a braggart and an unpopular character. If he didn't reclaim my belongings he'd be a laughing stock till his dying day. The operation would start at once and there'd be plenty of willing hands to help him. Hands to pull him up if he got into difficulties. Hands which would thrust him down the crack if he hesitated.

The old fool didn't hesitate. He was full of malt whisky and self-confidence and kept repeating his boasts. Alexander Selkirk feared nought, so what were we waiting for? What was delaying us?

There was very little delay. Fergus Bryde produced a rope and Brother Dan hitched their cart to the tractor. The wedded daughter made sure that liquor would be available and we climbed aboard for the fray. For some reason the dogs refused to join us, but who cared? We were all too drunk to care and superstitious fears had gone to the winds. If there was anything *nae canny* in the dungeons, brave Alex would settle its hash and report back. I think that most of the merry makers hoped he would find something unpleasant. I know that Dr Cayne was as cheerful as cricket as we rumbled across the moors. I believe that the Brydes sang 'Loch Lomond' loudly and tunelessly. I seem to remember slapping our hero on the back and saying he was a credit to the island.

We didn't travel by the direct route along which the dogs had harried me. Dan turned his tractor up a gentle slope that topped a hill and then wound down towards the cave. Our progress must have been visible and audible from the main road, but I wasn't worried that Kirk or Peggy or Moldon Mott might notice us. With the whisky warm in my guts I didn't give them a thought. The *Winsome Jean* had sailed long ago, but the trolls would give me a bed for the night and see me off on the morning ferry. A bit decayed perhaps but right as rain and as rich as Croesus.

The sun had started to go down when we reached Freda's shrine. The cave looked sinister and depressing in the twilight, but there's security in numbers and we had had plenty of booze for Dutch courage.

The hero of the hour seemed a bit green about the gills, but there was no going back. The rope was tied around his waist, someone gave him a torch and someone else gave him a helpful shove towards the fissure in the rocks. He vanished and Fergus unstoppered another bottle to drink his health.

I'd broken my watch during my own visit to the dungeons and I'd no idea how long it took Alexander to reach the bottom of the shaft, though it was a long way. At least a hundred and fifty feet was paid out before the rope stopped moving and then it jerked to signify he wished to come back. Bold Alex had found the rucksack and would soon be returning.

Fergus had given me the bottle and I drank from the neck and handed it to Cayne, but the doctor didn't take it. Danny Bryde interrupted him.

"The line jerked, but it's nae shiftin. The old devil's trapped, so give us a heave . . . All of youse . . . heave."

They heaved. Ten hefty hill farmers and daughter Flora tugged at the rope. They seemed to be hauling a lump of solid lead, but their labours were rewarded at last. The rope moved, though slowly. Inch by inch, Alexander Selkirk was dragged up from the stream and when he finally reappeared some lout started to sing *For he's a jolly good fellow.* I nearly joined in, because the rucksack was securely attached to his shoulders, but the song stopped abruptly. Daughter Flora screamed.

"I dinna ken him, I canna recognize him," she said after the screams ended and I sympathized with her because I couldn't recognize Selkirk myself. He was unrecognizable. Like the corpse in the dressing-gown, he hadn't got a face.

The police were naturally summoned and they arrived promptly. Kirk came with Gilespie and I was sorry to see him, but not too worried. The rucksack was safely on my own shoulders and I'd discarded his cairngorm camera by dropping it into the pool. I tried to appear unobtrusive while the trolls blearily explained the situation.

Alex Selkirk had got into difficulties and become wedged in the tunnel. He had died because his helpers had been over-zealous and the rope had crushed him against the rocks and torn most of his face away. In Gilespie's view the Fiscal might prefer manslaughter charges but Kirk doubted whether they would stick. A man had been slaughtered but with the best intentions. The rescuers had tried to save his life and it was sheer bad luck that he'd died in the process. Rather like pushing a suicide out of the path of a bus and into a lorry.

"A clear case of misadventure, Sergeant." The Brydes had kept quiet about my part leading to the events. Daniel said that Selkirk had made the climb for a bet and Kirk appeared to accept the statement. "Foolish for an elderly man to have attempted such a challenge, but we all have to die some day, as Mr Easter knows." He was bending over the corpse and gave me a cynical smile. "When the wine is in, the wit goes out, though no one can prosecute a man for being drunk on his own property. " He straightened and I saw him remove a shred of something from Alex's jacket. "Mr Bryde and his brother do not actually own the land of course, but they have a lease on the grazing rights and that should satisfy the Fiscal.

"No, I can't imagine that there's any reason why we should hang about here any longer, but please accept my sincere condolences, Madam." He bowed at the bereaved daughter Flora who had regained her composure and was probably thinking about *the bit put by* in the Linen Bank.

"There'll have to be an inquest of course, so get this unfortunate fellow taken down to the morgue. Use the Brydes' tractor and cart, Sergeant, and I'll borrow your Landrover and driver." I was pleased to see Gilespie wince, but my pleasure was short-lived. "Mr Easter and I have a deal of talking to do." He crooked his crooked hand at me and I followed him out of the cave.

"A deal of talking, Billy Boy, and, as I remarked earlier, confession is good for the soul."

Seventeen

Because of the driver Kirk didn't speak a word on the way to his bungalow and when we got there the first words I heard came from another source.

"You're safe, Bill?" Peggy opened the front door for us and smothered my face with damp kisses. "That maniac didn't harm you, Bill? Didn't attack you, darling?"

"What maniac, Peg?" The entire island seemed to be populated by lunatics and drunks, but none of them had actually assaulted me. "Who are you talking about?"

"Mott, of course. That beastly Moldon Mott." She was so overcome by emotion that I could hardly understand her, but Kirk told us to go into the sitting-room and calm down. Peg released my mouth and I got the gist of what had happened.

Unlike the major-general, Mott didn't trust me. He rightly imagined that if I got hold of the treasure I'd leave him in the lurch. He had hastened to Rhona to stop such an act of treachery. He had spotted Peggy leaving the castle grounds and followed her to the Hotel Mackenzie. He had stormed and threatened and, as usual, Peg had spilled the beans.

What she thought were the beans, of course. Peggy imagined that I intended to break into the castle itself, and didn't know about the underground stream or the dungeons. She had told Mott that I intended to search the house and recover his trophy and he believed her. He'd decided to waylay me after my search was completed.

"I've been so frightened, Bill. I was sure he had beaten you up and stolen the head . . . our head."

Peg sobbed and burbled. "Even without his wolves the man's a monster and capable of anything."

"My dear Peggy, Bill is also capable of anything and I'm quite sure he would be a match for Mr J. Moldon Mott." Kirk interrupted her diatribe. "As you can see, Bill's head is firmly on his neck where it belongs." He didn't know that she was referring to a different object which I'd hang on a hook in his hall. "Now, please keep quiet while I ask, and Bill answers a few questions.

"I know that Alexander Selkirk was not killed while he was being dragged through the stream and I believe I know what did kill him. I have no idea how you persuaded Selkirk to enter the dungeons, so let's start at the beginning.

"I want to hear a full account of what you discovered inside Inverlee Castle." He reached in his pocket and waved the photograph of the one-eared Bolshevik at me. "A very full account with particular reference to this man."

A full account? That's what the old fool asked for and that's what he got. The pail was not only full, but overflowing with inventions.

I described how I'd gained entry. A crafty ascent up a drain-pipe and in through a bedroom window. A cautious descent down the back stairs to the ground floor.

The sound of voices talking in some foreign language which I presumed was Russian. An armed guard stationed beside a door and more voices behind the door; Scottish voices. The family and their domestics held captive by the boorish Bolsheviks. I almost said that I'd heard Her Leddyship pleading for mercy and the swish of a knout, but thought that even Kirk wouldn't swallow that.

I did however say that I'd had a squint into a laboratory where Comrade Elfinovich must have prepared his mutated plant fertilizers and had been surprised by the great man himself.

My escape through the dungeons and up the stream with the Soviet hordes at my heels sounded enthralling. The only trouble was that I couldn't see how to fit Alex Selkirk in.

"Most vivid," Kirk said, grinning like a wicked uncle. "You are a compulsive story-teller, Bill, and might have made an honest living filling in the captions of a strip cartoon.

"A strip cartoon intended for retarded children." He turned and marched into the hall. When he came back the haversack was dangling in his grasp and his smile was triumphant. "No one over the mental age of six would believe such a pack of lies, but I'm not criticizing your mendacity.

"I'm a liar myself though a rather more plausible liar, Billy boy." He unzipped the bag and laid it on a table.

"Grigory Elfinovich, alias Rasputin. A character which never existed after 1916. I'll tell you who he really is later, but first things first."

"We must examine what Bill recovered from the dungeons, so keep your eyes skinned, Peggy." He reached inside the rucksack and chuckled.

"Abracadabra, my children." He was still chuckling when he grasped the contents, but the merriment soon ceased. Saul went to look for donkeys and discovered a kingdom. I'm not sure what Charlie Kirk hoped to discover, but the discovery surprised him and he dropped it. He dropped a heavy armoured helmet which rolled off the table top and thudded on his left foot.

"It exists then?" Though the major-general must have been in considerable pain he kept a stiff upper lip as he saw the glint of bright metal through the open visor. "You told me the truth under hallucinogenic drugs, Bill, and I'm duly grateful." He stooped and picked up the helmet, using more caution this time. "Canon Hendricks did bring his South American relic back to Rhona, and he decided on a suitable container."

"Where does a wise man hide a pebble . . . ? On a beach. Where does he conceal a leaf . . . ? In a forest." It took me a moment to realize he was cribbing from a Father Brown story. "Oliver Hendricks placed his head inside a head, but he must have opened it first I think." He had placed the helmet on the table and was squinting at it from several angles. "But how do we open the cocoon . . . the container? There must be a screw or a catch somewhere.

"And so there is." He drew out a metal pin and grinned. "Open Sesame, my friends." He flexed his fingers and the helmet did open. It opened on hinges and the thing inside was fully revealed. The yellow image of a man's face that glowed like a lamp on his mahogany table. "Allow me to present Don Francesco El Dracardo . . . the Dragon."

"Cor, ain't he lovely." Peggy was beside herself with joy, though I couldn't see anything very beautiful about the image. The features were rather like J. Moldon Mott's and there was more than arrogance and brutality about them. A hint of sickness and despair and I recalled my feelings in the dungeon; terror and panic. The blind awareness of something which Scots call *nae grue.*

"Keep your hands off it." Peggy had reached out to fondle the gleaming mask, but Kirk pushed her aside and carried the orb across to a wall safe. "No one is going to handle this joker till he's been treated by an expert, and that should be the expert now." His telephone was ringing, but he locked the thing away before taking the call. "General Kirk, here. Is that you, Professor?"

"Oh . . . Oh. The hospital, eh." His voice registered disappointment for a moment, but a brief moment. His fingers tightened on the receiver as he listened to the voice on the line and when he lowered the instrument he gave a long, low whistle.

"Well, well," he said. "The plot thickens and we must wend our way to the local infirmary." He buttoned up his jacket and wound the muffler around his neck. "Wonders never cease and Mr Moldon Mott has been ravaged."

The verb *to ravage* has several meanings, but to me it means sexual rape, and I didn't see how that could apply to J. Moldon Mott.

Kirk did not enlighten us. He sat brooding beside the police constable as the Landrover carried us to Drabster and only opened his mouth when he reached the quay. "Stop here, Officer, and I'll take the wheel." The evening ferry was just starting to tie up and he told the man to get out and wait for the passengers. It seemed that he was expecting some pal named Professor Top or Toup amongst the arrivals and the constable was to find a taxi to bring his pal along at the double. He let in the clutch and belted on.

"How could anyone rape Mr Mott, Bill?" Peggy shared my definition of the term. "Why should anyone want to?"

I told her that it took all sorts to make a world, which was why the world was in such a bloody mess, but I wasn't really interested in Mott's predicament. I could only think about my own stupidity and inaction. Kirk was an old man and he hadn't had a gun, so why . . . ?

Why hadn't I just laid him low when the helmet thudded on his toes and made off with its contents? Why had I allowed him to lock the relic away in his wall safe?

Not because of the tape recording of my confession. Not because of the police driver. We could easily have got out by the back door and scarpered across the heather. Not because Kirk implied the thing was dangerous. As an ex-soldier he probably knew about booby traps and high explosives, but nobody knew much about 'em when the thing was constructed. Though I hadn't cared for Don Francesco's appearance, his death mask wasn't a bomb which would blow up if you tampered with it. The orb was a golden shell stuffed with precious stones and worth a king's ransom.

So why wasn't the orb in my rucksack and on its way to the ferry from which Kirk's professor friend was supposed to be disembarking? Though the boat didn't return to the mainland till the following morning, I could probably have found an accommodating steward who'd give us a safe berth and send Gilespie and his men packing.

Why hadn't I? Why had I been so slow-witted? Why had I allowed Kirk to deprive me of a million-pound next egg and tuck it away in his safe?

I considered the questions while we lurched through the town and the answers came when Kirk drew up before the hospital. I hadn't been slow-witted, and I really did possess psychic powers. At the moment I saw that orb clearly I'd been warned to leave well alone. Francesco El Dracardo had died a long time ago, but I somehow knew that his spirit was alive and kicking.

"Is the blighter able to talk, Matron?" Kirk had been expected and with his customary agility he leapt out of the Landrover and hurried to a starched figure waiting on the hospital steps. "You're not going to tell me that he's dead?"

"The patient was alive six minutes ago and is in surgery." Matron shrugged and I distinctly heard her uniform creak. "He talked before the anaesthetic, but nothing he said made sense.

"Not to me, that is." She had a prim face which registered more disapproval than concern for Mott's welfare. "I have never been accustomed to foul language, General Kirk, and hadn't believed that such a torrent of abuse could issue from human lips.

"If Mr Mott is human, of course. X-rays showed that his skull is more like an ape's than a man's, and Doctor Mackie was astonished by the thickness of his cranium.

"That's why he's still alive, of course, but it's touch and go whether he'll survive the operation." The prospect of Mott perishing beneath the knife seemed to cheer her and she gave Kirk a sour smile. "I don't know why Doctor asked me to send for you, General. We were told to contact you regarding any more mysterious accidents, but there's no mystery in this case.

"The man was a prowler, and probably under the influence of drink. There was an empty hip flask of brandy in his pocket." She sniffed disapprovingly while leading us to a waiting-room. "Allan

Grant found him at the foot of Traitors' Leap, and it seems that he reeled or staggered over the cliffs in his drunken condition. A pity that he survived such a fall.

"I mean it is *a miracle he survived*, of course." She changed the statement hurriedly, but I knew that the first version had expressed her true feelings. "A fractured pelvis and cranium. A broken knee cap and three ribs gone." She listed Mott's injuries with relish. "One of the ribs may have penetrated a lung and that's why he's on the table now. Doctor Mackie's probing for splinters, but I doubt whether he'll get them out in time."

Matron might doubt. She definitely hoped that Mackie wouldn't manage to save J. Moldon Mott. I didn't blame her, but I had my own doubts. Not in regard to Mott's disablements. Not regarding his torrent of abuse when he'd been hauled to the hospital. The man deserved to be damaged, but what had caused the damage?

I might dislike Mott, but he was an expert rock climber and no fool. I'd bought a couple of his paperbacks in London and skimmed through 'em during the train journey north. *THE ASCENT OF MOUNT MOTT* proved the first point. *MANNERS AND CUSTOMS OF THE PAST* suggested he could hold his liquor and I recalled the start of one chapter.

"The Madagascans have no manners and their customs are disgusting. On arrival at Tamatava I was entertained by a group of aborigines who plied me with cups of a raw spirit distilled from lizard gall. They obviously hoped to get a white man drunk, but the attempt failed. It is a strong toper who can outdrink J. Moldon Mott."

Boasts, but not bare-faced lies. I was damned certain the contents of a hip flask wouldn't have intoxicated Mott and that he hadn't fallen down Traitors' Leap. He'd been pushed and I nodded when Kirk raised the same objection.

"You say that Mr Moldon Mott reeled over the cliff, Matron, which seems unlikely in my view, and on the telephone you used the term ravaged. A word hardly applicable to a mountaineering mishap. Will you explain exactly what you did mean?"

"It's difficult to be precise, General, but apart from broken bones which must have been caused by the fall, there were other factors. Most of his clothes had been torn and ripped off and there were lacerations." She paused to describe Mott's condition.

"Years ago, another patient with similar injuries was admitted here. The third mate of a ship that was unloading deck cargo. He'd been standing near a hawser and it snapped and caught him. His clothing was also torn to shreds and his body . . . That poor boy looked as though he'd been flogged with a steel whip."

"Thank you, Matron." Kirk nodded and turned to me. "Flogged with wires or clawed by an animal, perhaps?

"There have been several instances of animal savagery on this island, Bill, though not by wild animals. Dogs, cattle and pigs were the chief suspects and I wonder whether Mott encountered some such beast while he was waiting for you in the castle grounds?" Though the hospital was festooned with No-Smoking signs the general lit a cigar. "Could the unfortunate dupe you sent down the stream have had a similar encounter, my friend? Selkirk's face looked as though it had been torn by wires. Wires or claws or fangs."

"Selkirk was trapped in the tunnel and pulled out by force." I spoke with a confidence I didn't feel. "Pulled too hard and the rocks crushed him, and you saw that yourself. If you shone a torch down the stream you'd realize that no animal could have scrambled up from the dungeons. The climb is not difficult for a man, but one needs both hands to hold on."

"Possibly, Bill. We'll discuss the matter later, but here comes the Healer with the Knife." A door had opened and a youngish man in green overalls was walking towards us. "Let's hope he's managed to heal Moldon Mott."

"What news, Doctor Mackie?" Kirk raised his voice and his cigar. "Be he alive or be he dead?"

"The patient is living, General, though don't ask me why." The doctor's face was pallid with fatigue. "We've done the best we can and twenty-three bone fragments have been extracted, but we didn't save his life. He saved himself . . . That man's got the constitution of a horse."

Constitution of a horse . . . Skull like an ape's, I thought. Kirk had once said that several people had tried to kill me and failed. J. Moldon Mott seemed equally indestructible.

"He should pull through physically, but it's his sanity I'm worried about." Dr Mackie lowered himself onto a bench. "Patients often talk while under an anaesthetic, but this patient didn't just talk. He kept cursing and raving and in my view he may be committed to an asylum if he recovers."

"The nature of his ravings, Doctor?" Kirk's voice rasped as though he was interrogating a captured enemy agent. "The targets of his anger?"

"Two targets, General." Mackie considered the questions. "Mr Mott abused a man he called Judas Easter. He seemed to think that some woman had pushed him over the cliff.

"No, he didn't name the woman, but managed to give a description." The doctor was looking at Kirk and had hardly noticed our presence. "A garbled description, of course, but he said what he'd do if he found her.

"She-Devil," he kept repeating. "God help that devil when I get hold of her. Bitch . . . bloated, red-headed bitch." Mackie noticed Peggy and his eyes almost popped out of their sockets. "That bloated, scarlet Jezebel sank her teeth into me."

"It wasn't me. I've never bitten any one in my life. I didn't shove Mott over any cliff." The doctor had departed, Matron had placed a private office at our disposal, Peggy was quivering with fear and indignation. "Bloated, scarlet Jezebel indeed. How could he have said such a thing? How can you suspect me, General Kirk?

"I didn't go near the castle again. After Mott left me at the hotel I was frightened for Bill's sake and I took a taxi and went to your bungalow. You know that, General. You let me in and when the police telephoned you told me to wait there and I stayed put. Surely you remember that?"

"Naturally, Peggy." Kirk appeared unimpressed by her injured innocence. "But while I was with Gilespie on the hill you had ample time to go the castle grounds and dispose of Mr Mott before I returned.

"You also had ample motives for wishing him dead. To assist your partner and take revenge on Mott's bullying tactics. I suspect you have a violent streak in your nature and I'm sure Bill could confirm that opinion." He looked at me for confirmation, but I didn't respond. Though Peg had assaulted me more than once, it's a dirty bird that fouls its own nest, however foul the nest may be already.

"Ample motivation . . . ample time, and ample strength at your disposal." Kirk eyed her thoughtfully. "Bloated is not a word I should use to describe a lady, but we can't deny that you're a fine figure of a woman and an exceptionally powerful one.

"Motivation and means. Time and identification." He was still eyeing her fine figure and then pointed his cigar at her gingery mop. "Scarlet Jezebel. Red hair and should we put it more politely . . . size.

"If Mr Mott regains sanity and repeats his identification, Gilespie and the Fiscal may have some very troublesome questions to ask. At the moment I have a simple request." He stood up and reached in his breast pocket. "Will you allow me to examine your hair, Peggy?"

"Thank you." She had nodded and he held something against her head and smiled. "You may have noticed this in the cave, Bill. A strand of reddish hair which I removed from Alexander Selkirk's jacket. A strand which was probably shed by Selkirk's murderer or the creature which killed him."

"Evidence which proves Peggy completely innocent." He tucked the evidence back in his pocket and patted Peg on her shoulder. "Though the colours match, your good lady's locks are soft and luxuriant while my specimen is coarse and stringy.

"Not Peggy's hair I'm glad to say, but, as Moldon Mott said during the operation, the hair of a She-Devil." He pulled at his cigar stub and blew a smoke ring. "You consider that no animal could have climbed up the stream, Bill, but one animal might have managed it.

"I think we're looking for some creature with a reddish pelt, an evil temper and a pair of strong hands. Maybe The Old Man of the Trees, as the Burmese call him.

"In this instance, The Old Lady of Rhona."

Eighteen

The Old Man of the Trees! The old fool from Army Intelligence was barking up the wrong tree, as usual. Kirk's statement was rubbish.

Orang-outangs, male or female, get their nickname because they look old and they are arboreal creatures who live in forests. To the best of my knowledge there wasn't a forest near Traitors' Leap. There were definitely no trees growing in the dungeons. It was possible that a tame orang might have been kept as a pet in the castle, of course. Both Rudyard Kipling and Edgar Allan Poe wrote stories testifying to the animals' loyalty and devotion. Also to their murderous tendencies when aroused. An orang-outang could easily have attacked Mott or Selkirk, but Mott wouldn't have survived the attack. The animal's strength is seven times greater than a man's and he'd have been pulled apart.

Finally, no *Pongo pigmaeus*, to use their generic name, could survive a cold northern climate without warm accommodation and supplies of fresh fruit. That meant that the Stuart-Vails and their retainers had been keeping the beast, and knew what it was up to. I didn't believe that even clannish loyalty would stretch that far.

"I accept your knowledge of the ape world, Bill, but what do you know about loyalty?" I'd told Kirk that I'd visited Borneo and studied the habits of *Pongo pigmaeus*, but he interrupted. "Allan and Molly Grant are not merely family retainers, they are appendages of the family and regard their employees as demigods. In former days, each child on the estate had to swear an oath of allegiance to the head of the clan, upon his tenth birthday." The general stubbed out the butt of his cigar.

"Allan served under a pal of mine when he was in the army. He was a brave and devoted soldier, but my friend believes that Allan's loyalty to the clan came before the crown."

"But orang-outangs don't swear oaths, General." Now that

Peggy had been exonerated she accepted my logic. "They're mean, treacherous brutes and liable to turn on any one; even their owners. I've seen 'em in zoos and they're horrible looking creatures. No one . . . Not even Moldon Mott could mistake 'em for women."

"I said *maybe* an orang-outang, my dear, and we must wait and see what Mr Mott has to say if he regains consciousness. In the meanwhile have you a better theory to offer, Bill? I was speaking figuratively when I mentioned the Old Man or Old Woman of the Trees, but where do you imagine this came from?" He pulled out the tuft of hair for my inspection, but I didn't want to inspect it. I had questions to put to Charlie Kirk.

There were no Soviet agents at Inverlee Castle. Grigory Elfinovich, alias Rasputin, was an invention, so whom had I seen in that dungeon? Who was the recent corpse in pyjamas and dressing-gown?

"You did find him, Bill." The old boy didn't answer the question, but he looked pleased. "The truth at last, though I'm sorry you didn't tell me earlier.

"I am also sorry I couldn't confide in you earlier, but it was impossible." He tucked the hairs away and smiled. "You wanted that golden relic, and you're a brave man, Billy. A gang of Bolsheviks wouldn't have stopped your quest. You were prepared for natural hazards, but you have a deep respect for other forces. Powers which you cannot understand.

"The sinister Soviets spreading plant mutations to drive men and animals mad. A dangerous task to get past them, but greed made the gamble worthwhile. I dealt the cards and hoped you would accept the joker I offered. Which you did, Billy . . . Yes, you did.

"You welcomed my help to enter the castle. We helped each other, and I regret that I couldn't tell you the truth earlier. A great deal of harm might have been avoided, but every cloud has a silver lining. A golden lining in this instance. Dracardo's head is yours to take if you still want it, and there is only one condition." The smile vanished and his tone grew as cold as the ice which probably filled his brain. "You must return to those dungeons, Bill, and deliver a proper report."

"To hell with you, Charles Kirk." Of course I wanted the orb, but wild horses wouldn't send me down to the pit again. I cursed his offer when we were interrupted.

"Ah, there you are, Charles." There had been a brisk rap on the door and a brisk woman strode into the room. "Sorry for the delay, but blame your bungling British transport system. Never have I experienced such inefficiency."

Kirk introduced us. His visitor was Frau Professor Gerda Toppe and I gathered she was top of the class in some specialized field of knowledge, but they didn't say what field. We shook hands and she delivered a tirade against the United Kingdom and all its works.

"An hour's delay leaving Leon, almost four hours at Rio. The B.A. officials said there was a suspected case of *Legionnaires Disease* on board. Utter tosh. The man had a heavy cold, but would they listen to me?

"Not on your Nellie." The Frau Professor had a broad face which resembled a boxer's; a Boxer dog's. "Pshaw!!" She used an expletivc that I'd never actually heard spoken though I knew it registered contempt. "I should have been here yesterday, but more time was lost on the flight. The pilot stated that adverse winds were responsible . . . He lied.

"Poor engine maintenance, and amateur navigation held us back. No more shall I travel on one of your aeroplanes, Charles. For me it shall always be *Lufthansa*." Indignant sentences but they told me a great deal about Professor Toppe. She had recently returned from South America. She was connected with the medical profession. She was a Kraut and a damned arrogant one.

"And if that was not bad enough they lost my luggage on the ferry. Nincompoops . . . Dunderheads . . . Jacks in Office.

"However, I have arrived at last, and no more time must be wasted. Got your notes with you?" It was a command rather than a question and Kirk opened his brief-case and produced a wad of typescript. "Good . . . Got a gasper?" She sat down at a desk and scowled when Kirk offered her cigar case. "No, not one of those damned things. I want a cigarette . . . a fag. For some reason the boat had run out of smokes . . . Typical.

"Ta!" She accepted a Silk Cut from me, but failed to see the joke when I struck a match and said, "A Lucifer to light your fag, Madam."

"*Herr Gott!* No taste at all." She pulled off the filter tip and sucked the paper tube. "At home I smoke *Rot Handen* (Extra Strong). May die of cancer, but so what. A short life and a merry one. Jump laughing into my grave." A remark attributed to the late Colonel Adolf Eichmann, but I don't believe he laughed at the end. "Ahah . . . Ahah!" Frau Toppe had donned a pair of spectacles which made her look rather like Heinrich Himmler and appeared pleased with Kirk's file. "Excellent, Charles. Twenty-seven attacks on animals. Ten on human beings and that does not include this Moldon Mott or the man in the cave.

"Policemen and hospital staff have tongues, Madam, and I would be glad if you would hold yours till I've finished." Peg had enquired how she knew about Mott and Selkirk, but the professor spoke as though sentencing her to a concentration camp.

"Yes, thirty-nine assaults and over half of them fatal." The total seemed to have restored her good humour. "A very creditable score and you were quite right to consult me, but . . ." She had turned a page with a nicotine-stained fingernail and frowned. "But why is this? You needed a dupe to enter the castle and do the dirty work. You selected Mr Easter and fed him a . . ." She paused to think of an apt phrase and settled for *Bull and Cock story.*

"Very prudent, Charles, but these notes are incomplete. I must know exactly what Mr Easter discovered." She paused again and jabbed her yellow finger at me. "Tell me what you saw, Mr Easter. I wish to hear from the mouth of the horse."

I told her. I told the atrocious woman everything or almost everything. What had I to lose? The head was in Kirk's safe. The tape recording was on its way to his solicitor. I'd lost the lot and I described my visit to the dungeons. How I'd spotted Rasputin's body and knocked over the suit of armour. How I'd panicked and had to abandon the rucksack and the helmet. How Alexander Selkirk had volunteered to recover my property and died in the attempt. I didn't say how Alex died because I didn't know, and Madam Toppe didn't appear interested. She cut me short and turned to Kirk.

"Grigory Elfinovich Rasputin! I presume that was a joke, Charles. If so, it is in poor taste." She removed her Himmler spectacles and dragged at the mutilated cigarette. "The man you saw in the prison was almost certainly Spangel . . . Doctor Hans Spangel. Does that toll a bell, Mr Easter?"

A bell didn't actually toll, but the name produced a faint clink, Spangel was an East German who had defected while attending some conference in London. After a deal of political wrangling he was granted asylum, but vanished some months later. Rumour had it that he'd been abducted and forcibly returned to the bosom of his Fatherland, but no one was sure.

"Partly right . . . mainly wrong, Mr Easter." Toppe gave the desk an impatient rap. "Spangel did defect from the East German People's Republic. He was granted asylum in Great Britain." She made it sound as if he'd contracted pox. "Spangel did disappear, but he was not abducted. As General Kirk has since discovered, Hans Spangel came to Rhona of his own free will. Spangel was paid to visit this island because he had knowledge to sell. Doctor Spangel was a genetic engineer."

Genetic engineer? She had used the term impressively, and though I'm not a scientist, the bell did toll. Genetic engineering . . . Messing about with the chromosomes . . . Altering the hormone balance . . . Changing the entire nervous system and the bodily system too . . . Producing mutants.

That could explain the events on Rhona. If Hans Spangel had not been a bona-fide defector, but an enemy within the gates, he might have spread the tares which drove men and animals mad. If he hadn't been killed, the island's population might have decided on a mass exodus to the mainland. If the Stuart-Vails and their retainers were under Spangel's thumb they might have cited George the Third's edict and assumed sovereignty of the island. Red flags might be waving over the Atlantic.

"That was what I originally suspected, Bill." I'd voiced my theory and Kirk nodded. "And not only genetic changes. Aberrations of the social patterns too. An orang-outang deserts the trees and roams under an open sky. A friendly dog turns killer. If a man was subjected to Spangel's treatment he might become an unpleasant man and that's why I invented Comrade Elfinovich.

"You braved the K.G.B. to recover that head, Bill, but I don't think you'd have risked genetic transformation. To have ended up as a freak . . . A sub-human monster."

"Bosh, Charles. You are still shilly-shallying." Though Professor Toppe had a fair command of the English language it was a somewhat archaic command and she delivered more outdated comments and then rose to her feet. "Stand still, Mr Easter. I wish to examine you." She grabbed me by the chin and peered into my eyes.

"Nothing yet. Nothing apparent but the process takes time. Hours or days pass before the deformity is revealed, so open your mouth wide." Though I did not like Gerda Toppe, though her fingers were digging into my flesh, I did what she ordered and put out my tongue. The terms had scared me stiff and I yielded to her inspection.

"Why . . . why didn't you warn the young man, Charles? Deformity is what we must consider, though Mr Easter appears untouched so far." She let me go, but kept staring at my face as though I was a leper.

"I am by profession a teratologist, Mr Easter, a student of monstrosities and monstrous births and for your own sake you must tell me the truth.

"Did you open that golden ball, Mr Easter? Did you see what El Dracardo's death mask really contains?"

Nineteen

"So the Devil did look after his own, Bill." I'd sworn that I hadn't opened the orb and Kirk sounded relieved. "You are a lucky man, my boy. If greed had overcome prudence you might have had to be . . ."

"Lucky or blessed with the powers of survival, Charles." Gerda Toppe interrupted him. She appeared satisfied with my physical condition and glanced at his notes. "We have no such intuitive aids however and must marshal the facts." She proceeded to marshal them, tapping the pages with a pencil.

"Moldon Mott locates the relic up the Selva River and Canon Hendricks steals it from him and returns to England. Hendricks brings his trophy to this island in the belief that it possesses an evil influence which can be removed by the water of some trumpery British saint.

"Oliver Hendricks left the thing on Rhona, but we do not know how many people were allowed to examine it. However, we know that on his return to England he committed a series of motiveless murders before seeking sanctuary in the Smeatons' flat.

"Oliver Hendricks or Henry Oliver, as he called himself, had died of natural causes when Mr Easter disposed of his corpse." She paused and gave me an approving smile. "That was a most creditable piece of work, but I only wish credit was due in an another quarter." She frowned at the notes and then at Kirk. "You harnessed the cart in front of the horse, Charles, and the sequences are wrong.

"*Dummer Kern . . . Dumkoff . . . Lumpen Handler.*" She abused the major-general in German and then showed that he had indeed been a *Dummer Kern* . . . A very foolish fellow.

Because Hans Spangel, the defector, had been a genetic engineer, Charlie Kirk had put two and two together and discovered they added up to five. In Kirk's view, Spangel had mutated the flowers of the field and driven the beasts of the field crazy. Spangel had hoped to depopulate the island and force Lady Elizabeth to hand over Rhona to the Ruskis. Poor, old Hans Spangel was responsible for all the current ills. Poor, old Charlie Kirk had spent six months on his worthless theories. In three days I'd proved that his sums were wrong. Another mathematician was needed. Gerda Toppe who had been consulted earlier received a further appeal for help. She had hastened from Leon and was now prepared to demolish Kirk's card house.

Spangel had disappeared from London *after* the Stuart-Vail family went into purdah. Spangel reached Rhona *after* the first outbreaks of animal savagery were reported. Spangel was dead and his watch showed that he'd died months ago. Spangel was a victim and General Charles Kirk had been barking at the wrong hole again.

Barking! The word made me think of how the dogs had barked while I walked from the Thistle Inn. How the hill had echoed with their crazed baying and howling. How I'd realized that there was something evil in the castle dungeons.

Something hellish! The last memory was so vivid that I hardly noticed the phone ring or saw Kirk answer it. I heard him bang down the receiver, however and address Toppe in confident tones.

"I may have been wrong on one or two minor points, Gerda, but I stand by my guns." After the way she'd talked, I felt he hadn't got a foot let alone a gun to stand by, but he sounded unabashed.

"It seems that Mr Moldon Mott is coming out of the anaesthetic and may be able to speak soon. I don't know what he'll have to say, but think we should visit him."

Assuredly they should. The professor had moved to the door as Kirk completed the sentence, but we were not invited to the pow-wow with Mott. "You and Peggy will stay here and keep out of mischief, Bill." As I didn't have the combination of his safe and didn't want to see that damned head again I couldn't imagine what mischief to get up to, but I nodded as the old buster marched away, slamming the door behind him.

"Quiet, Bill." Peg was peering into a glass fronted cupboard, and she motioned me to join her. "Look what's in here."

I looked but I couldn't see anything of interest. The cupboard seemed to contain an assortment of medicines and I asked Peggy what she had in mind.

"You need courage, Bill." She opened the case and reached for a bottle of mauve-coloured tablets. "To be taken only in instances of acute depression, anxiety and bereavement." She read the label aloud and handed me the bottle. "Swallow five of these, Bill. I know what they are and they won't hurt you.

"Please, darling." I also knew what they were and hesitated. "That Toppe woman tried to scare you, but there's nothing to harm us inside that head. She and Kirk want the treasure themselves. They're a pair of crooked liars, but we'll get the better of 'em.

"Good." I had swallowed five Purple Hearts and she produced other, larger bottles. "Charcoal tablets for wind in the stomach. A solution for treating gout. A cure for constipation. Look at what the active ingredients, Bill. Surely you understand?"

She held the bottles up and I did understand. Every fun-loving school boy has been told that gunpowder is composed of three elements. Charcoal, potassium and sulphur and the elements were listed on each prescription. We had the means to blow up a headmaster and I felt like blowing one up as we crept out of the hospital.

I wasn't sure whether chemicals adulterated by other substances would react as strongly as in their raw state, but I was pretty certain they'd make an effective bang. A powerful bang which would rip Kirk's safe open or fling it from the wall.

The amphetamine pills had started to give me confidence and anxiety was a thing of the past. I forgot Toppe's mention of deformity and only technical problems remained. Would Mott manage to keep Kirk and the professor occupied till we were on our way? What was the position regarding Kirk's transport? How could we get to the bungalow?

Needless anxieties. Mott was garrulous and had plenty to say. Kirk was senile and neglectful. He'd neglected to remove the key from the Landrover. The engine fired at a single twist and we set off to reclaim our treasure.

Worse luck! How I wish that the engine had not fired or that the policeman had returned to his vehicle. How I curse Mrs Peggy Tey. Her rashness, her Purple Hearts and her knowledge of chemistry.

Twenty

Our first spot of trouble was to bump into a troll and his dog. Not one of our own trolls fortunately; I'd already begun to think of the Brydes as personal friends. I didn't recognize the troll who stopped us for some time and I didn't actually bump into him but over him.

The night was dark and cloudy. Mist was rising from the ground to obscure the headlamps and I was driving fast. I didn't know the troll was there, but I saw the dog standing on the crown of the road. I honked my horn, but it didn't budge, so I swerved left to avoid it. An operation which saved the dog, and jolted the Rover. The inside tyre made contact with a larger object, and we landed in the ditch.

Not a serious mishap. With four-wheel drive I could easily have backed out and was doing so when Peg suddenly screeched and pointed at the thing that had dislodged us.

The dog had made off and a man was lying on the verge. A dead man, but the collision hadn't killed him. Landrovers are excellent vehicles, but not war chariots. No scythes or knives are fitted to their rims as optional extras and our troll looked as though a circle of swirling blades had caught him.

We climbed down to examine the victim more closely. I considered two of Kirk's earlier statements.

That a brace of Scottish retainers would defend their hereditary masters in the teeth of all comers. That the said retainers had transferred their allegiance to the Bolsheviks and were holding the master or rather mistress (Lady Elizabeth Stuart-Vail) captive in her own castle.

Conflicting theories, but there was little doubt what had happened to the troll, and when I had examined his face I saw the dog turn and snarl at us.

One retainer might have resisted the teeth of all comers and teeth appeared to have killed him. Allan Grant had pocketed his last florin.

We were not responsible for the bailiff's demise and we didn't waste time. I reversed out of the ditch and drove on with Peggy's comforting hand on my thigh. Drove more slowly, though I was damned pleased when Kirk's bungalow hove into sight.

The door was locked, of course, but I smashed a panel with a stone, reached for the knob of the Yale lock and we stepped inside.

"The curtains, Peggy." I waited for her to draw 'em before switching on the sitting-room lights. Though the explosion we planned would probably blow out of the windows as well as the drapes, I didn't want any officious eyes viewing our preparations.

"Good!" We were decently screened and I looked for a receptacle to house our charge. Kirk's silver cigar box seemed suitable because the lid had a strong spring catch and an engraved inscription to add a personal touch. "Presented to the *Chief* (Major-General Charles Kirk) by the officers of Section 18 (British Army Intelligence Corps)." I mentally thanked Section 18, tipped out the *chief's* Coronas and got to work on his presentation while Peggy mixed the ingredients.

Gunpowder is not widely used as an explosive today, but it's effective enough if the force is contained and the cigar box should be just the thing. I found a pocket knife and a ball of twine on Kirk's desk and had punctured a hole in his trophy when the lights went out. The old sod didn't want anyone using his electricity when he wasn't in residence and had installed a slot meter.

I found the meter without difficulty, but we had only two ten pence pieces between us and they wouldn't last long, though long enough. The safe wasn't as soundly constructed as I'd imagined and one charge should blow it open, but Peggy thought we should keep enough materials back for a second attempt if the first failed. I agreed, slipped the twine through the hole in the box and knotted it.

Kirk had also installed an independent source of heat and there was a paraffin stove in the kitchen. After I'd given the cord a thorough soaking, Peggy had completed her chemistry experiments and we filled our home-made bomb and looked for a heavy object to hold it in place. An easy choice, because the bookcase was on castors. I trundled it across to the safe, Peggy wedged the box home and our preparations were completed.

I was pretty certain that one charge would be sufficient, but there were ample supplies for another attempt and more than enough sulphur. Only ten per cent is used in the production of gunpowder and one of the jars was still almost full. Peggy replaced them in her bag and we went into the kitchen and closed the door. Sulphur burns like hell and we didn't want any flash back touching it off. I struck a match, lit the end of the twine and we waited.

We only had waited a few seconds, but they seemed like hours. Though the cord had been thoroughly treated with paraffin and flared satisfactorily, it was a slow, flabby flame which travelled at a snail's pace. After it vanished under the door Peggy imagined our fuse had gone out and suggested I should open up and have a look.

Mercifully I didn't. The door suddenly shot back of its own accord or rather on account of the explosion. A formidable explosion. The shock wave threw me against the kitchen sink and after I pulled myself together I couldn't see anything for a moment. Most of the lamp bulbs had been shattered and the bungalow was filled with a thick, lilac-coloured fog which blanketed our vision.

A mist that slowly dispersed because the front windows had vanished, but an acrid stench remained and I was coughing when I stumbled into the sitting-room.

The gunpowder had made a fine mess of Kirk's library. The book case was shattered and heavy volumes lay strewn on the floor. I heard Peggy curse and drop her bag as she tripped over one of them. I think she warned me not to strike a match as the sulphur jar might have been broken but the warning was unnecessary. I was certain that the safe door must have been buckled and I'd borrowed a screwdriver from the Landrover's tool kit as a jemmy. We'd need no more bombs and I'd strike no more matches in that bungalow. The next match I'd strike would be to light a cigarette when we were safely on our way.

With our treasure . . . ours to take. The safe door had been buckled and yellow metal was glinting through the gap. A gap which was wide enough for the screwdriver blade to gain a purchase and I drove it home and heaved. The steel groaned in protest, but came away eventually. I laid aside the jemmy and for the first time my fingers touched the golden head of Francesco El Dracardo. For the second time Peg voiced her admiration. "Cor, ain't he lovely?"

An asinine remark and I realized just how asinine when I laid the thing on Kirk's table. Don Francesco might have been an imposing man when alive, but there was something wrong with his death mask. The surface was blurred as though his artist had neglected to shave him before taking the impression and the features were distorted and thickened. They made me think of a medical term which refers to leprosy and other objectionable diseases . . . Lion-faced.

But it wasn't El Dracardo's appearance that disappointed me. The relic itself was wrong and I nearly followed Kirk's example and let it fall on my foot.

The metal glistened brightly enough, but the glisten wasn't warm and soft and sensuous. It was fairly heavy, but not heavy enough. I know a great deal about gold and the casing was not gold. I told Peggy that we'd got ourselves a load of brass which might be saleable to a collector of historical items, for a few pounds.

"Never mind the casing, it's the jewels inside that matter, Bill." Peggy may have shared my initial disappointment, but she didn't give up hope. "All them precious diamonds and emeralds and pearls." I hadn't heard that any pearls were listed, but her imagination was running riot. "Sapphires and rubies and amethysts."

"Open it, Bill. Someone may have heard the explosion and there's no time to lose. Either open it up or we'll take the whole thing along with us." She tilted her bag upside down to make room for our trophy. I saw a quantity of sulphur fall onto the carpet, but I hardly noticed it. I'd seen something else to arouse my interest.

Though most of the image was blurred and rough, the forehead was unwrinkled apart from five lines carved on the brass. Lines of letters, too small to be legible by the naked eye, but I grabbed a magnifying-glass from Kirk's desk and craned over the inscription.

"Inter hoc conditorio situm is spiritus Dracardo et quis custodiet." The words were Latin . . . Medieval monk Latin, and though I'm not a classical scholar I could attempt a rough translation, "In this tomb or coffin . . ." I wasn't sure what *conditorio* actually meant, but it was either a casket or a burial place . . . "lie the spirit of Dracardo and that which guards him.

"My treasure is for God and Saint Peter to release my soul. My lips are closed to cage the devil. Open those lips and learn the power and fear of the dog. Let me rest and avoid damnation."

"The lips . . . the lips, Bill." Before I could finish the inscription Peggy had grabbed the screwdriver and thrust it into the metal mouth. One hefty wrench and the lips did open. The whole of the casing slid in two and we saw the treasure of Francesco El Dracardo.

A treasure for God . . . the cage of a Devil. I forgot the mention of a guardian. I forgot everything . . . I just stared in wonder as God's gifts sparkled at us.

Diamonds glittered through a maze of dark hair. Emeralds clung to mummified flesh and blackened bone. Two gigantic rubies glowed from the eye sockets.

Inter hoc conditorio. The inscription made sense at last. The orb was a treasure chest. It was also a tomb and a coffin. The coffin of a man who had died long ago and left God a legacy. His own head cut off from the nape and sealed in metal.

Sealed with precious stones to placate Saint Peter, though I didn't know why. I didn't know that the inscription ended with a warning. I didn't know why Don Francesco had feared dogs or what was his guardian.

I just stared at those glowing ruby eyes till the lights went out.

Damn Kirk for having a slot meter fitted. Damn me for having no coin to feed the meter. Damn Peggy for dropping her bag and breaking the sulphur jar. I was just about to strike a match when I remembered the sulphur. We'd have to work in the dark and I told Peg to hold the bag open on the table.

I groped for our repulsive, mummified, but extremely valuable find. I winced as I touched the mass of hair which seemed to wrap itself around my fingers. I winced far more when I heard voices.

Peggy was right. The explosion had been noticed and we were not alone.

"Wha . . . Lah . . . Tha." The voices were speaking . . . trying to speak. The owners of the voices were walking along the passage . . . trying to walk. As they entered the sitting-room a cloud slid away from the moon and I saw their shadows. Four or five distorted images bent like hoops and much larger than the shadows of human beings.

"Cahr . . . Har . . . Wha . . ." The moonlight was obscured again, the shadows vanished and I can't describe what the voices sounded like. Try to imagine a dog talking and it might give you a clue, but not a normal dog. Not domesticated Fido, the Family Friend. Every syllable had a growl and a snarl and a threat in it, and though I couldn't see the interlopers I could smell them. A rank, musty smell far stronger than the reek of gunpowder. A stench which reminded me of Smeaton's flat and though my leg muscles were paralysed by fear, I blurted out a question. "Who are you?"

"Tha . . . Da—damed . . . do-domed . . . Tha hun . . . tered . . ." Four or five of them, and terror increased my mental activity. I've heard that drowning men re-live their entire lives at the moment of death. I don't know whether that's true, but I know that I re-lived several days in less than a minute.

I pictured the vast, hairy corpse of Oliver Hendricks as I trussed him on his bed. I remembered what we had learned from Bishop Hurst Hutchins, and what Moldon Mott had said about El Dracardo. I knew why Dr Hans Spangel had been summoned to Rhona.

Not to spread sickness, but to cure the sick. The doctor had failed and his patients had killed him.

The farm animals had been driven mad because other animals were roaming the island. Don Francesco's head had been sealed in brass because it did contain a guardian. A force which had sent Canon Hendricks off on his murderous journey. Which had led to the strange events on Rhona and kept Lady Elizabeth and her brothers out of sight.

Out of sight, but not out of mind. For over a year Allan Grant and his wife had minded their feudal masters, but the masters and the mistress had emerged from the dungeons from time to time and an age-old myth became reality.

Possibly Grant had decided that loyalty had to stop, and died accordingly. Maybe he had just happened to be in the way of his charges. Probably . . .

Possibly—probably—perhaps? Unimportant questions and there was no time to consider them. I had to consider our predicament, because the legend was no longer a fairy tale to frighten children.

Our companions were were-wolves.

Twenty-one

Lycanthropy is a mental illness in which a human being imagines he is a wild animal. The probable cause is inferiority and the subject often identifies himself with a wolf, because wolves were once mankind's most formidable foes.

The creatures in Kirk's bungalow did not suffer from lycanthropy, however. They were actual werewolves because Francesco El Dracardo had been mainly a wolf. His mummified head housed the spores of a disease which created physical as well as mental aberrations. Dormant spores that had remained alive but inactive till Oliver Hendricks opened the box of mischief and moisture and oxygen wakened them.

I didn't know that at the time, of course. Professor Toppe explained the germ cycle later, but the disease is a form of *Hypertricosis* (abnormal hairyness) and it has several other symptoms. The jaws, fingers and the entire muscular system are strengthened and deformed. The brain runs riot.

The subject not only believes he is a beast, he becomes one, but still retains human cunning and intelligence. Oliver Hendricks, a former clergyman, killed his victims on holy days, and concealed his traces by mutilating the bodies with man-made instruments. His fellow sufferers did not bother to take such precautions. They regarded the island as their private preserve. Inverlee Castle as their lair. The Grants as their keepers and protectors. They roamed their kingdom and the terror began.

It seems that the condition may be halted if one is lucky. Provided our own defence mechanisms, the anti-bodies, rally they destroy the microbes though some of the scars remain. Hendricks had almost recovered when he took refuge in Smeaton's flat, but he still craved for food. He still feared a wolf's natural enemy, the dog. A fear which was reciprocated. The very presence of the man-beasts drove animals insane. The crazed howling and the outbreaks of savagery were accounted for, though domestic animals didn't savage Mr Gordon, Alexander Selkirk, J. Moldon Mott or Hector Grant. Lady Elizabeth Stuart-Vail and her brothers got hold of 'em.

There are many other strange factors about the illness, but I didn't consider them while we cowered in the darkness. All the creatures were in the room now and one of them giggled; a sort of giggle. I could smell their breath as well as their bodies; a sort of smell. I knew they could see in the dark and had seen us. I could hear them creeping towards us. I realized we would die obscenely unless appropriate action was taken, but what action?

"The kitchen." Peggy had tugged my arm, but I ignored her. The kitchen offered a temporary refuge, but there must be a better way; there was. The enemy were almost within arm's reach when Saint Paul in his wisdom came to my aid. I might die painfully, but at least my death would be hygienic.

"Better to marry than burn." Some people say that that remark suggests Paul hated women. They may be right, but I hated one woman. I hated the Lady of Rhona and it was far better to burn than fall into her clutches.

I reached for my matchbox and struck a light.

I knew that sulphur is highly inflammable, but I didn't realize how inflammable or how attractive the combustion can be when viewed from a safe distance. As the match reached the carpet we belted back through the kitchen door. There was a slight sizzling noise and then came the inferno.

Tongues of lavender-coloured flame rose from the floor and I saw our companions clearly. They were naked, but covered with thick matted hair resembling cloaks like the woman Gordon encountered at the shrine. Hair which started to smoulder and appeared strangely fungoid in the grey-blue light and though its owners stood on their feet they were definitely not men and women. A female voice screamed, but not as a woman screams. A male voice bellowed in anguish, but not human anguish.

Their reaction was purely animal, and they didn't seem to realize what was happening at first. They howled and gibbered and tore at the flames with their claws and then beat a panic-stricken retreat down the corridor. Buffeting each other, snarling at each other as they stumbled out to safety.

And we had to find safety too. I had defeated the living menace, but the friendly fires had become enemies now and the blaze was spreading. The whole bungalow would soon be alight and the back door from the kitchen was locked. Our only hope was to follow the foes and we followed. We soaked two towels with water, covered our faces and groped through the flames to Mother Nature.

Mother Nature turned up trumps. She laid on a sudden torrent of rain which dampened our clothes and then stopped abruptly. A wind blew from the west, the cloud cleared and when I'd pulled off my towel I saw five figures moving away up the fells.

Moving quickly—shambling and stumbling through the heather, but not quickly enough. Not nearly as fast as the river rushing to meet 'em.

A river which rippled rather than flowed across the moor and each ripple had a brain and a single aim in life. To take life and destroy an age-old enemy. The dogs were after blood and we watched 'em get it.

The Battle of Rhona didn't last long. Most of the island's canine population had joined forces and no energy was wasted in barking or growling. The army swept down in silence till the slaughter commenced.

I think I saw the Brydes' Grip and Grapple in the vanguard, but I can't be sure; the pack were too numerous. Collie and terrier—greyhound and lurcher—labrador, mongrel and Alsatian. Every type of dog seemed to be present and every dog intended to have its day.

If the werewolves hadn't revolted me so much I might have sympathized with them, but I was past caring and the action was too brief to take in details. I think I heard a single half-human bellow of fury. I believe I saw one huge, deformed figure struggling to break free, before a dozen jaws dragged him down and he vanished under the weight of numbers.

After a few minutes the strife was o'er and the war won. The vanquished lay dead. The victors melted away to homestead and kennel.

A few more minutes passed and then a cavalcade of motor vehicles arrived. General Kirk climbed out of a car and glowered at his blazing bungalow. Sergeant Gilespie produced a pair of handcuffs and glowered at me.

Twenty-two

Tape Recording made by Major-General Charles Kirk

Mrs Tey has been discharged from hospital, but William Easter must remain in custody for his own good and the good of the public. The happenings on Rhona must also remain secret in the public interest. Though every member of the Stuart-Vail family perished, panic is a dangerous force and it has been decided to treat the events as classified information.

Poor Bill! Should he survive his tribulations and issue an account it is bound to be garbled and inaccurate. Though he once visited the Selva River, Bill knew little about the life and death of Don Francesco El Dracardo and ignorance is costing him. *Break in text as narrator chuckles and lights a cigar.*

"Don Francesco was more than an explorer and a conqueror. Like many men of that age, he dabbled in alchemy and herbalism and it seems that the second subject caused his terrible end. Consumption of the fungus, *Mycelium selva*, led to delusions. Like the founders of Rome, he began to believe he was descended from wolves and drank the blood of *Lyciscus lupus*, a creature indigenous to the the Selva area.

Micro-biology was an unknown science in the 16th century and Dracardo could hardly have realized that such rashness made him the victim of a hideous disease. He probably imagined he was possessed by a demon, and when his followers decided he had become unfit to live he accepted death on certain conditions. The executioners were to cut off his head and seal it in a brass casket, so that the evil spirit could never escape before the day of judgement. Precious stones must also be lodged inside the container. Gifts to appease Saint Peter at the gates of Heaven.

"Supposition, of course, but Gerda Toppe felt sure that the Dracardo head contained a dangerous medical agent, and Moldon Mott probably shared her view. We'll hear from Mott ere long, but now to my own involvement." A second break in the text as the general is heard pouring himself a drink.

"I had often visited Rhona for the grouse shooting and formed an acquaintanceship with Lady Elizabeth and her family. Whilst dining at the castle one evening I realized that something was amiss. My hosts quite literally wolfed their food and Oliver Hendricks appeared panic-stricken when he heard a dog barking outside the windows.

"An unpleasant evening and before returning to London I questioned Allan Grant and learned that all the other servants had been recently dismissed for no apparent reason and he and his wife were the only staff at Inverlee Castle. Grant was reticent, but hinted that Oliver Hendricks had brought something with him from South America. Something which was disturbing his employers.

"I gave the matter little thought. It all seemed unimportant till I learned that Oliver was suspected of being the Mad Vicar and had disappeared. That aroused my curiosity as I'd always regarded Oliver as a basically harmless individual and I discussed the case with a Scotland Yard superintendent, who is a member of my club.

"From him I learned that the Vicar could not have used Rhona as a hiding-place after the murders as the mainland police had checked all persons visiting or returning from the island once suspicion fell on Hendricks.

"The next point to interest me was a letter from Sergeant Gilespie, who served under my command during the Korean War. Though Jock Gilespie was born in the Hebrides he is not given to flights of fancy, but the communication showed that he was disturbed by the outbreaks of animal violence. He also mentioned that Lady Elizabeth and her brothers had gone into seclusion when the first Vicar murder was committed and never appeared in public.

"My third informant was a former subordinate at Army Intelligence who was investigating the disappearance of Hans Spangel, the East German defector. Apparently Spangel had taken a train to

Scotland shortly before he vanished." Another break and a sound which might be raindrops or the clicking of Kirk's tongue.

"I admit that I got the time factors wrong, but my premise was basically correct. Hans Spangel was a genetic engineer, so could he be responsible for the events on Rhona? A luncheon with Gerda Toppe, who happened to be in London at the time, convinced me that Spangel could.

"I also learned from Toppe that certain genetic disorders are not passed by the microbe itself, but by spores which had recently been revived by air or moisture. To risk the bite of an infected individual would be extremely rash and dangerous.

"Poor Bill Easter has discovered how rash." More chuckles and a creak of chair springs interrupt the tape briefly.

"I felt it my duty to return to Rhona and investigate the situation and the Minister of Defence gave his blessing. Jock Gilespie arranged for me to rent the bungalow, and in my role of holiday resident I could remain unobtrusive but exert official influence."

"Again I admit that I was slightly wrong and followed a false scent for some time. I firmly believed that Hans Spangel was the culprit. That he had won over the Grants and their employers and was responsible for the animal aberrations. The truth, of course, was quite different, as Mrs Molly Grant has since confessed.

"Oliver Hendricks opened the casket and showed the contents to his relatives. They all became infected and Grant must have realized what was happening. Allan Grant appealed to Spangel, the great genetic engineer, to treat his charges and Spangel probably did his best, though the best was not good enough. He failed and was killed accordingly, but the Grants' misguided loyalty persisted. Allan and Molly screened their werewolves, and Allan paid for his devotion. Molly isn't sure why they turned on their protector in the end. Molly wasn't very rational. It's unlikely that she'll ever be released from an asylum.

"No, I made little progress till Bill Easter and Peggy Tey fell into my lap, and Bill told me so much under the influence of pentothal. I learned about Hendricks . . . I learned about Moldon Mott and the South American treasure. I put two and two together and, despite Bill's opinion, they added up to four.

"Bill's arrival was like a gift from the gods, and he was more than just a source of information. He is a thoroughly bad and expendable human being, but a useful tool in the right hands, and though one of my hands is crippled I know how to use it.

"Comrade Grigory Elfinovich! I invented the name to test Bill's gullibility. It was a long time before he thought of Rasputin, and when he did, he imagined I was a senile dotard. Bill decided to play ball with me for his own interests.

"Interests which I shared. Telephone conversations with Gerda Toppe had convinced me that El Dracardo's head might be the trouble.

"Rasputin . . . Hah-hah-hah. An orang-utang . . . He-he-he. Bill Easter would never have entered that cave if he'd realized the truth, but he's realizing it now, and I feel slightly sorry for him.

"Not unduly sorry, however. Professor Toppe assures me that the condition can be cured, if treated in its early stages, and Bill is receiving treatment while I dictate this. A rather painful process based on electric convulsions and strychnine injections, but his sufferings must be borne.

"Though the bungalow was totally destroyed by fire, it was a rented property and my personal chattels were insured. Things have turned out splendidly and the curse of Rhona is lifted.

"Also, much has been gained, because fire could not destroy the orb's other contents, and I have arranged that justice shall be done.

"What the hell is that?" Kirk's voice is interrupted by the sound of hammering. "Told the receptionist I wasn't to be disturbed. Abominable service, but I'd better see who it is I suppose." Kirk pauses though his footsteps are heard moving to the door.

"Quite abominable. Report the manager to the highest quarters." *Creak of door opening and recording ends with a single word.*

"You . . ."

CONTINUED NARRATIVE OF WILLIAM EASTER

"Yes, me, Charlie Kirk." I marched into the room, switched off the cassette machine and scowled at the pitiful bastard who cringed away as well he might.

While Kirk had been comfortably ensconced in his hotel I'd suffered torment. I won't describe what torments; they're indescribable. Muscular spasms akin to cramp—intense thirst and a craving for blood. If I hadn't been strapped to a bed I'd have bitten the first nurse available.

For three weeks I'd been tied to that damned bed with contacts fixed to my arm and the needle in waiting. God knows how many electric shocks and strychnine injections they gave me before Professor Toppe blandly declared that Peggy and I had been saved by her skill and devotion and were out of danger.

Physical torture was over . . . Mental torment remained. I had to recuperate and was wheeled into a ward containing another recuperator, J. Moldon Mott, who was still heavily bandaged, but his own revolting self again.

One hour of the man's boasts and abuse convinced me that I could stand no more and I scarpered.

My clothes had been impounded, but I found a pair of overalls and boots in a porter's cupboard, and nobody saw me leave the Gestapo H.Q. I wandered through Drabster to recover my stolen property and punish the thief.

The Royal Goat is the island's best hotel and it seemed likely that I'd find my quarry there . . . I did. The girl at the reception desk told me the old brute's room number, but said he'd left strict orders not to be disturbed. I went up by the service lift and hammered at his door. My instinct assured me that the old brute must have pocketed the jewels after the fire was extinguished. My emotions suggested that Professor Toppe was both right and wrong. I might not be a danger to the public in general, but I was a danger to a general officer and the gallant officer realized his danger.

"You, Bill. They've let you out and you're completely cured and free from infection." Though he spoke like the hypocrite he was, his body was trembling with abject fear. "Thank God, my boy, or rather thank Frau Toppe. She gave you the treatment in time, and all's well that ends well."

"Cu—cred . . . Fre-fe. Nevere." I attempted to reproduce the voices I'd heard in his bungalow. ("Not cu-red . . . got let out. Ru-run out . . . loped out, gotter a way.") The act flopped, but I bared my teeth and tried to look threatening. "Need something . . . Need blood, Charlie Kirk. Your blood . . . Good red, salty blood."

"Stop being foolish, Bill." Both performances had failed and his confidence returned. "You are perfectly sane and healthy, but you need a drink, so sit down while I fetch one." I accepted his offer and lowered myself into a chair while he poured out whisky and water. "No Mickey Finn this time, my friend. Drugs are quite unnecessary, because you've sung your swan song on Rhona." He carried a glass across to me and raised his own. "To prosperity, Bill. One mission is completed, but I'm sure there'll be more. He who schemes and runs away, lives to scheme another day.

"Now, to business. You feel that I did you and Peggy a disservice. That I gambled with your lives, and you're right, of course, though I acted in the best interests." He picked up his brief-case and produced two battered, blackened pieces of metal.

"Your Dracardo head, Billy Boy. I'm afraid it was rather damaged when the roof of the bungalow collapsed, but it should be an interesting memento of our joint victory.

"You can handle it freely. Fire is the best method of sterilizers, and the spore tissue has been rendered harmless."

"Stop hedging, General Kirk." If I hadn't been so weak and dispirited I'd have slung the pieces of brass at him. "These are worth nothing, and what have you done with the real treasure? Those rubies and emeralds and diamonds?"

"Worth nothing, Bill? Once again I saw his eyebrows form a bar across his forehead. "You are too pessimistic. I don't know the current price of brass, but a scrap dealer should pay you a fiver for those, and the legal owners have no objection to such a sale."

A fiver! I'd been thinking of a million pounds and repeated my question. Where were the jewels? What had he done with the loot?

"The loot. What vulgar terminology, my boy. The loot, as you call it, is in safe-keeping and will be delivered to its proper owners in due course. Sergeant Gilespie's men searched the bungalow with a fine tooth comb, and everything of real value has been recovered. Here is an inventory of what they did find." He held out a sheet of typed paper. "The estimate was done by a local jeweller, I'm afraid, and the Procurator Fiscal instructed him to make a conservative estimate. We don't want to raise the owners' hopes."

The owners? I didn't know who he was referring to, but when I glanced at the list my own hopes soared. The loot was worth far more than I'd imagined. Those worthless pieces of brass had once held a king's ransom.

"*Diamonds* (80). of Brazilian origin and twelve exceed one hundred hundred carats. VALUE (estimated) £350,000."

"*Rubies* (2). Same origin and both of exceptional size and quality. VALUE (est) £500,000."

"*Emeralds* (36). Obviously mined in the region of Columbia. All compare favourably with the finest known examples of this important gem stone. VALUE ???.

"We are unable to put a price upon the last item. In our unprejudiced opinion the total collection submitted to us by General Charles Kirk and Colonel Sir Andrew Gow (Procurator Fiscal of the Outer Isles) should fetch no less than two million pounds if offered for sale at any reputable public auction.

Yours faithfully . . ."

An indecipherable scribble below and the names and address of the faithful above. *Haldane, Huxley and Marx, 19 High Street, Drabster.*

Two million! Old Kirk had turned out trumps after all. Though the Fiscal had the hoard under lock and key, I'd recovered it and could afford to be generous. A three-way split between General Charlie, Sir Andy Gow and myself. Messrs Haldane, Huxley and Marx could also have a small cut if they kept their mouths shut.

"A split, Bill! Are you suggesting that Colonel Gow, Mr Huxley or myself are criminals?" Kirk clicked his tongue sadly. "All these items must naturally be returned to their proper owners, who may be prepared to offer some further token as a reward for your services." He looked at the two sheets of brass on the floor. "They have already promised to make a generous donation towards a project which Colonel Gow and I hold very dear. We intend to purchase Inverlee Castle and convert the building into a home of rest for retired gentlefolk on fixed incomes."

"A donation!" I knew who the first guests would be and my mind boggled. Two former officers of the British Army were preparing to hand over a couple of million quid to a hostile dictatorship. The rulers of Nuevo Leon might subscribe a pittance towards their geriatrics' home, but only a pittance, and thirty pieces of silver was the usual price. The bulk would be spent on printing presses and guns. Propaganda to attack the United States and Western Europe. Firearms to keep their downtrodden serfs in line.

"Leon, Bill?" I was about to mention a great many other things on which the money could be spent, but he raised his horrible, grey hand and cut me short. "I do hope your memory has not been impaired. The dictators of Leon were disposed of some time ago and the United Nations controls the country now.

"I suppose Moldon Mott has a sort of claim, but I don't think he'll make one. What evidence is there that he found the relic before Hendricks? Only his own word and possession is nine tenths of the law. Mr Mott made a poor impression on me and he won't impress a judge more favourably. Mott is a non-starter legally, though I'm sure the rightful owners will offer him some compensation to avoid unpleasantness.

"Quiet, retiring people. Bill. You told me how much they dislike publicity."

I couldn't recall telling him anything of the kind. I didn't know who he was talking about. If he was referring to the Stuart-Vails he'd better consult a psychiatrist. They were dead, and I'd seen 'em die.

"Of course you don't remember what was said, Bill. You were under the influence of pentothal. I've already apologized for that and I'm sure there are no hard feelings." He delved into his case again and produced a second sheet of typescript. "Your statements have enabled me to see that justice shall be done."

There were hard feelings and if there was any justice knocking about Kirk would have joined the werewolves in a blaze of sulphur, but I took the paper from him and frowned. It appeared to be a photocopy of some legal document full of technical jargon, which solicitors use to bewilder their clients.

"In return for the aforementioned presents, the Party of the

Second Part (hereinafter referred to as the Second Party) promises the First Parties to fulfil and observe the following conditions and this Agreement shall be equally binding upon his heirs, executors and assigns.

"To keep the interior of the demised premises and its fixtures and fitting in good, decorative order.

"To store no inflammable substances upon the said premises which might invalidate the First Parties' insurance cover."

It took me a moment to realize the thing was a tenancy contract. My hand shook when I understood the terms of the contract. My heart pounded when I saw who the tenant was and what he had agreed.

The tenant wanted sanctuary and he'd signed away a fortune, though his landlords had not known the fortune existed till old Kirk maliciously put his oar in.

"If, for any reason, the Second Party withholds the said rent, his portable goods and chattels shall become the absolute property of the First Parties and this agreement shall remain binding after death."

The tenant was Henry Oliver or Oliver Hendricks. You can guess who the First Parties were. You cannot imagine my feelings. I'd slaved and suffered torment. I'd risked life and limb and sanity for two people I thoroughly despised.

For Mr and Mrs A. K. Smeaton, c/o The National Central Bank, Feltonford, Bucks.

ALSO AVAILABLE FROM VALANCOURT BOOKS

Michael Arlen	Hell! said the Duchess
R. C. Ashby (Ruby Ferguson)	He Arrived at Dusk
Frank Baker	The Birds
Charles Beaumont	The Hunger and Other Stories
David Benedictus	The Fourth of June
Charles Birkin	The Smell of Evil
John Blackburn	A Scent of New-Mown Hay
	Broken Boy
	Blue Octavo
	The Flame and the Wind
	Nothing but the Night
	Bury Him Darkly
	The Face of the Lion
Thomas Blackburn	The Feast of the Wolf
John Braine	Room at the Top
	The Vodi
R. Chetwynd-Hayes	The Monster Club
Basil Copper	The Great White Space
	Necropolis
Hunter Davies	Body Charge
Jennifer Dawson	The Ha-Ha
Barry England	Figures in a Landscape
Ronald Fraser	Flower Phantoms
Gillian Freeman	The Liberty Man
	The Leather Boys
	The Leader
Stephen Gilbert	Bombardier
	Monkeyface
	The Burnaby Experiments
	Ratman's Notebooks
Martyn Goff	The Youngest Director
Stephen Gregory	The Cormorant
Thomas Hinde	Mr. Nicholas
	The Day the Call Came
Claude Houghton	I Am Jonathan Scrivener
	This Was Ivor Trent
Gerald Kersh	Nightshade and Damnations
	Fowlers End
Francis King	Never Again
	An Air That Kills
	The Dividing Stream
	The Dark Glasses

C.H.B. Kitchin	Ten Pollitt Place
	The Book of Life
Hilda Lewis	The Witch and the Priest
John Lodwick	Brother Death
Kenneth Martin	Aubade
Michael Nelson	Knock or Ring
	A Room in Chelsea Square
Beverley Nichols	Crazy Pavements
Oliver Onions	The Hand of Kornelius Voyt
J.B. Priestley	Benighted
	The Doomsday Men
	The Other Place
	The Magicians
	The Thirty-First of June
	The Shapes of Sleep
	Saturn Over the Water
Peter Prince	Play Things
Piers Paul Read	Monk Dawson
Forrest Reid	Following Darkness
	The Spring Song
	Brian Westby
	The Tom Barber Trilogy
	Denis Bracknel
George Sims	Sleep No More
	The Last Best Friend
Andrew Sinclair	The Facts in the Case of E.A. Poe
	The Raker
Colin Spencer	Panic
David Storey	Radcliffe
	Pasmore
	Saville
Russell Thorndike	The Slype
	The Master of the Macabre
John Wain	Hurry on Down
	The Smaller Sky
	Strike the Father Dead
	A Winter in the Hills
Keith Waterhouse	There is a Happy Land
	Billy Liar
Colin Wilson	Ritual in the Dark
	Man Without a Shadow
	The World of Violence
	The Philosopher's Stone
	The God of the Labyrinth

Lightning Source UK Ltd.
Milton Keynes UK
UKOW02f1417230117
292668UK00002B/144/P

9 781939 140845